# THE RECENT WIDOWER

*Amish Romance*

## BRENDA MAXFIELD

*Tica House*
*Publishing*

Sweet Romance that Delights and Enchants!

Copyright © 2022 by Tica House Publishing LLC

All rights reserved.

No part of this book may be reproduced in any form or by any electronic or mechanical means, including information storage and retrieval systems, without written permission from the author, except for the use of brief quotations in a book review.

# Personal Word from the Author

**Dearest Readers,**

Thank you so much for choosing one of my books. I am proud to be a part of the team of writers at Tica House Publishing who work joyfully to bring you stories of hope, faith, courage, and love. Your kind words and loving readership are deeply appreciated.

I would like to personally invite you to sign up for updates and to become part of our **Exclusive Reader Club**—it's completely Free to join! We'd love to welcome you!

**Much love,**

**Brenda Maxfield**

BRENDA MAXFIELD

**VISIT HERE to Join our Reader's Club and to Receive Tica House Updates!**

https://amish.subscribemenow.com/

# Contents

| | |
|---|---|
| Personal Word from the Author | 1 |
| Chapter 1 | 5 |
| Chapter 2 | 16 |
| Chapter 3 | 20 |
| Chapter 4 | 31 |
| Chapter 5 | 36 |
| Chapter 6 | 46 |
| Chapter 7 | 56 |
| Chapter 8 | 71 |
| Chapter 9 | 80 |
| Chapter 10 | 94 |
| Chapter 11 | 107 |
| Chapter 12 | 116 |
| Chapter 13 | 128 |
| Chapter 14 | 136 |
| Chapter 15 | 151 |
| Chapter 16 | 158 |
| Chapter 17 | 172 |
| Chapter 18 | 181 |
| Chapter 19 | 193 |
| Chapter 20 | 204 |
| Chapter 21 | 217 |
| Chapter 22 | 229 |
| Chapter 23 | 239 |
| Chapter 24 | 257 |
| Chapter 25 | 267 |
| Chapter 26 | 279 |
| Chapter 27 | 293 |
| Epilogue | 296 |

| | |
|---|---|
| Continue Reading... | 301 |
| Thank you for Reading | 304 |
| More Amish Romance for You | 305 |
| About the Author | 307 |

# Chapter One

> Behold, I will do a new thing; now it shall spring forth; shall ye not know it? I will even make a way in the wilderness, and rivers in the desert.
>
> — ISAIAH 43:19 KJV

"Cornelia, *please* stop bothering your brother," Josh Lambright said, reaching over and pressing his five-year-old daughter's hands back to her lap.

"But *Dat,* he's botherin' me."

"*Nee,* I ain't," complained David, who was four.

Josh sighed heavily, weary beyond words. If only Sara was still here. She would be able to calm the children. She had such an easy way with them; she made it look simple.

But it was anything but simple, as Josh now knew. Being both father and mother to his two children was proving beyond his capabilities. Thus, this move. He leaned back against the vinyl seat of the hired van, his thoughts morosely latching again onto his sorry life of late.

He wondered whether this move had been the best decision, but it was too late to change his mind now. The few belongings they still possessed were in boxes in the back of the van. His two children were sitting to the right of him in the back seat, and the driver in front was focused on the road ahead, humming under his breath. They'd been riding for hours and hours now, and Josh despaired of ever reaching Hollybrook, Indiana.

"How much farther, *Dat*?" Cornelia asked, her plaintive voice matching his mood.

"I gotta go to the bathroom," David piped up.

"You just went," Cornelia scolded him. "*Dat* said we can't be stopping every five minutes."

"This ain't five minutes," David countered.

"That's enough, *kinner*," Josh said. He looked down at David's huge brown eyes. "Do you really have to go?"

"I gotta go," David said, frowning.

"Charles," Josh said, stretching forward to speak to the driver.

"I heard him," Charles replied. "It's no problem. I'll pull off the freeway up ahead."

"Thank you." Josh looked again at David. "Just hold it a bit longer. We're going to stop."

David nodded and stuck the first two fingers of his right hand into his mouth—something he did when he got nervous or upset. And in truth, he'd been sucking those two fingers a lot lately. Josh sighed again. *Sara, why did you have to leave us?*

A ridiculous question. Sara hadn't purposely fallen from the barn loft. She hadn't purposely broken her neck.

He shuddered, as he did every time he thought of it. He could still clearly see her twisted body splayed out on the barn floor. He could still hear Cornelia shrieking frantically that, "*Mamm* won't get up!" He could still feel Sara's limp body in his arms when he knew it was too late, and Sara was never going to get up again.

David tugged on Josh's sleeve. "I really gotta go."

"I know, son. We're turning off right now. You can go at the gas station."

David sucked hard on his fingers again, looking worriedly out the window.

"He's sucking his fingers again," Cornelia reported. "David, only *bopplis* suck their fingers."

"That's enough, Cornelia," Josh said.

"Here you go, young man," George said as he pulled into a large parking space in front of a convenience store at the gas station.

David was already fumbling with the seat belt, trying to free himself from the booster seat. Josh helped him. Cornelia also unbuckled herself.

"Can I come in, too?" she asked. "I'll go potty, too."

"Let's all go," Josh said, opening the door. He got out and helped his two children down, and they all walked into the store together.

~

Two hours later, George turned the van into Josh's mother's place, down the long drive toward the expansive white farmhouse. The wide porch wrapped around the front of the house to the right side all the way to the back corner. Josh had spent many hours on that porch during his growing up years, and it looked exactly the same—from the porch swing, the two rocking chairs on each side of it, down to the huge wooden pot that held sprawling ivy.

"We're here?" Cornelia asked.

"Where's *Mammi*?" David asked, straining to peer out the window.

"She'll be out in a minute, if I know your *mammi*," Josh said. He was eager to see his mother. His father had died only four months before, an exact month after Sara's death. Josh hadn't been able to come see his mother then, though he'd wanted to; there was simply too much to deal with so soon after Sara's death. And he'd been overwhelmed with dealing with it all, not the least of which was his two grieving children. Thus, he was eager to see his mother now. More than eager.

George was already out of the driver's seat and had come around to open the back of the van to get at their boxes. Josh helped his children from the van, frowning. Hadn't his mother heard them pull up? She was expecting them. It was odd; why hadn't she at least come out to stand on the porch to welcome them as she always did?

Cornelia and David were already running toward the porch. Josh hurried to help George with the boxes when he heard the screen door bang shut. He exhaled in relief and looked toward the porch. Tamar Lambright had appeared, and she was holding her arms out to her grandchildren. But seeing her was a punch to Josh's stomach.

She looked old. Ancient, in fact. Where was the mother he remembered, who bounded about even at the age of seventy? He flinched and watched her for a moment, noting her thin arms and her hunched stance. What had happened to her? It hadn't been that long since they'd seen her.

But he was wrong; it had been a long time—nearly a year. Could such a change have occurred in a mere year?

Or was it his father's death that caused such a stark transformation? Guilt soared through him. He should have made more of an effort to come home for the funeral. He should have slogged through his own fog of grief and bewilderment to come.

He sucked in a huge breath. Well, he was here now, wasn't he?

His mother looked over the heads of her grandchildren, and her eyes locked with his. Even at this distance, he saw the sadness there, the tears welling. He put down the box he was holding and rushed to her. He enveloped her in his strong arms and held her close. He was stunned at how fragile she felt in his arms. Why, she would blow away in a stiff breeze.

"You're home, son," she said, patting his back. "You're home."

He drew away to look down at her lined face. "I'm home now, *Mamm*."

George was toting two of their boxes to the porch.

"*Ach*, George. Let me help you with those." Josh let go of his mother and hurried to help. It wouldn't take long; there were only nine boxes. He'd left everything else they'd owned in the house. It went to the new owner, a young man who'd just married his sweetheart. The two of them had been overjoyed to inherit all of Josh's belongings. Josh's *and* Sara's.

Josh had brought one of Sara's *kapps* with him. It was folded neatly in the middle of his box of clothes. He had to keep something of hers, and this *kapp* still smelled like the shampoo she used. He'd spent more than one evening all alone by the warming stove with that *kapp* in his hands. He couldn't bear to leave it behind even though her scent was fading.

How could he make the *kapp* retain her aroma? He wished he had that power.

But of course, he was being ridiculous. He was a grown man with two children to raise. And now he was here to farm his father's fields.

He and George finished unloading the boxes, and George took off. Josh had expected his mother to ask the Mennonite driver in for supper, but she didn't. This, too, was odd. He drew in a long breath. Maybe he and the *kinner* being there would help things get back to normal.

But when he entered his childhood home, he knew things would never be normal again. The house looked the same, more or less, but it felt like a different home altogether. He paused just inside the front door. He realized he was waiting for his father's booming greeting. He was waiting for his father's heavy footsteps and ready smile. He was waiting for some silly joke his father had heard just the other day.

But instead, all he heard were his children's excited chatter and his mother's cooing responses. He swallowed past the growing lump in his throat. He'd known it would be hard to come home when his father was gone, but he hadn't known it would feel like a physical blow.

"Where are we gonna sleep, *Mammi*?" Cornelia asked.

"I don't wanna sleep with Cornelia," David stated.

"I have made up the two beds in the room next to mine," Tamar told them. "You'll be together for the time being."

David made a face at Cornelia, but Cornelia wasn't looking. She had spotted a tub of wooden toys in the corner of the front room.

"Look, David," she cried. "Toys."

They both took off across the room and dove into the toys.

"I s'pose I'd better bring the boxes in," Josh told his mother.

She nodded, looking a bit lost.

"Am I to sleep in my old room?"

She nodded again. "I thought you'd like that."

"It's fine, *Mamm*." He hesitated, feeling the need to say something more. Feeling the need to somehow console his mother, but he felt empty. He was scraping bottom himself, with nothing left to give. He scowled, annoyed with himself. He took in a deep breath. "I can help you make supper."

It was a sad offer, but the best he could do. His mother gave him a watery smile.

"You'll do no such thing," she said, her voice faltering only slightly. "I'm still able to put a meal on the table."

"*Ach*, of course, you are, *Mamm*. I never meant—"

"I know," she interrupted him. "And thank you."

She offered a thin smile and walked away toward the kitchen. He went outside and stood for a moment on the porch, inhaling deeply. Sara was gone. She was not coming back. He had to accept it and go on. He shook his head. Wasn't that the reason he was here? He *was* going on. And if he and his mother could help each other on their way, then so much the better.

But it wasn't going to work out as he'd assumed it would. His mother wasn't doing well. Even in the few moments they'd been together, he could see that. His father's death had shaken her to her roots. She wasn't the same. But then, why would he have possibly thought she would be the same? He wasn't the same after losing Sara. He wasn't the same at all.

Before taking in the boxes, he went down the porch steps and toward the barn. He needed to see how things stood around the farm. He could tell by glancing that he had his work cut out for him. He wondered at the finances. He had made some money selling off his farm, but he had held a mortgage, so his proceeds hadn't been as much as he would have liked. Still, if he combined them with his father's finances, they should be able to make it just fine.

He paused at the door of the barn and gazed behind the house at the stretching fields. He needed to get the soybeans planted, and it was already past time. It should still be all right, though, but he needed to get on it right away.

Did his mother have the stamina to watch Cornelia and David all day long? He'd thought it would be fine, but now, he wasn't so sure. In truth, he wasn't sure at all. Cornelia hadn't yet started school, for she'd only recently turned five. She could start in the fall. But that wouldn't help right now.

He went inside the barn and walked over to the plow, slowing running his hand over the blade. His father had always kept his farm equipment in top condition, and it still showed. He gazed over at the plough horse who was watching him placidly from his stall.

"Crafty," he said affectionately. "You still here? You outlived your master, didn't you?" He walked over to the horse and rubbed her nose. "Next time, I'll bring out a carrot or two. Would that suit?"

He smiled and patted the horse's neck. Things looked more or less in place which relieved some of his concern. But now, he should get back inside. His Cornelia was an active one, and he didn't want her wearing out his mother the first hour they were here.

He gave Crafty one last pat and headed back for the house. He didn't even reach the porch before Cornelia came blasting out through the screen door.

"*Mammi* says she's got kitties," she cried, racing by him.

He caught her arm, and Cornelia came to a screeching halt.

"*Dat.* Let go. I gotta go see the kitties."

"And you shall. But slow down a little, will you? Is your brother coming?"

"*Nee,* he's with *Mammi* in the kitchen." She gave her father an exasperated look. "Who wouldn't want to see kitties?" she asked. "Don't make a bit of sense."

Josh had to laugh at that. He let go of his daughter's arm, and she flew off toward the barn. Goodness, but that child could wear a person out. Could wear anyone out, truth be told. What had he been thinking to bring her to his mother? Maybe he could hire someone—someone to help around the house and to help watch his children. He'd discuss it with his mother after the children were settled into bed that very evening.

# Chapter Two

Lucy Oyer wiped the last drip off the counter. She stood back and surveyed the kitchen. Every single thing was in place and spotless. She knew better than to leave it otherwise; she'd gotten quite skilled at ensuring every room in the house was perfect.

Otherwise, she'd pay for it. Without thinking, her hand went to her left ear. Her hearing still wasn't right in that ear. After her father had hit her, the pain had been excruciating. She'd nearly passed out—but she hadn't dared. That would have only made things worse. So she'd stood, leaning heavily against the kitchen table, trembling while he'd berated her clean-up job. When he'd finally huffed out of the room, she'd collapsed on the floor where she'd stayed for a long time.

She kept reaching up to her ear, expecting blood to be pouring from it. But there hadn't been any blood. Just piercing pain. And now, two months later, her ear still wasn't right.

She glanced again at the kitchen, making double, triple sure it was fine. And then she went down to the basement. It was Monday—laundry day. In truth, she and her father didn't produce much laundry in a week. One time, a couple years before, Lucy had gotten the bright idea to skip laundry day until the next week. It had made perfect sense to her; it would save her the labor that day and she'd simply do a fuller load the next week.

It did not make sense to Bartholomew Oyer.

Lucy never made that mistake again.

It was spring, so the basement wasn't too cold. When she was young and her mother was still alive, she didn't like the basement. It gave her the shivers. She told her mother that monsters lived there. Her mother had laughed and then grabbed her hand and taken her down there. Janet Oyer had lit five lanterns, and they had searched every corner of the basement for monsters. Of course, they didn't find any.

"See, my little Lucy?" her mother had said. "There are no monsters here. Not a single one."

"But, *Mamm*, maybe they're hiding," Lucy had countered.

Her mother had pondered this with great seriousness. "Maybe," she said. "And if so, then they're afraid of you."

Lucy had never thought of it that way, and she was highly relieved. Her mother could always make her feel better. Always.

It was only years later she realized there was a monster living in their house, just not in the basement. Lucy felt guilty for thinking such a thing about her own father, but it was true. She didn't remember him being so cruel when her mother was still alive. But since her death five years before, he'd gotten progressively worse. At first, Lucy had tried talking to him, crying, begging him not to be so mean. But it had only enraged him further.

So now, they lived in peace as long as Lucy did everything exactly the way he liked it. She lived with constant dread he'd find something wrong, something to berate her for—or if it was truly bad enough in his eyes, something to hit her for.

But he never came down to the basement, which was puzzling. But she was happy for it. Working in the basement was now one of her favorite things to do. It had become a haven of sorts. Once, she'd decided to do all the mending down in the basement, but that hadn't gone over well. Her father called her back up, demanding to know why she was down there in the evening.

"You need to tend the warming stove," he told her sharply. "You need to stay up here come evenings."

It puzzled her for her father was the one who fed the stove. Could it be he was lonely upstairs by himself? That he wanted her close by? The thought was jolting to be sure. She didn't explore the idea too thoroughly because it was upsetting. But she didn't take the mending to the basement again.

She dreamed sometimes of getting away from her father—of escaping and going somewhere else. Somewhere she didn't have to walk about on eggshells. Somewhere she could be herself. Somewhere safe. But how could she survive? If she tried to go to kin—and there weren't many kin in the first place close enough to make that possible—her father would only come and fetch her back. And he'd be angry, and things would be worse.

What she needed was some kind of job. She was well into her twenties, more than old enough for a job. She needed something where she could make enough money to live. Then maybe she'd have a chance. She wouldn't need her father then. The very thought made her shiver with possibilities. If only it could be true... But she'd played the "if only" game so many, many times, and she never got anywhere. She was accustomed to having her dreams dashed; she was resigned to it.

But someday ... *someday*, she would have an out. And when she did, she was going to make very, very sure she never allowed any man to have such power over her again.

# Chapter Three

Josh tucked the light quilt under Cornelia's chin.

"This bed don't feel right," she muttered, already half asleep.

"You'll get used to it," he said gently, patting her auburn curls. "Why, in no time at all, it'll feel just like home."

"We ain't goin' back?"

"*Nee,* daughter. We ain't going back."

She went very still. For a moment, he thought she'd gone to sleep but then, she stirred.

"*Dat?*"

"*Jah?*"

"*Mamm* won't know where we are. What if she comes lookin' for us?"

Josh sucked in a deep breath. "*Mamm's* in heaven. You know that. She won't come lookin' for us."

"But you said she was lookin' down on me. 'Member? You said, she was watching me with love."

And so he had. "I did say that."

"So now, she'll be looking for me at our old house. She won't be knowing we moved to *Mammi's*."

Josh felt his chest constrict. Dear Lord, but he didn't know what to say sometimes. Sara would have known. It would've been better if his two children had lost their father, not their mother. And then a wave of guilt washed over him. It wasn't his place to question the ways of God.

"She'll know, Cornelia. She'll know."

"But how?"

"You'll tell her. Or *Gott* will tell her." He perked up. That was a good answer.

"I better tell her right now. And I better tell *Gott*." Before he could say more, she scrambled out of bed and knelt beside it. "*Gott?* You there? Will you tell my *mamm* that I'm here at *Mammi's* now? I don't want her lookin' for me at our old house. And tell her that I'm not liking my bed as much here. Will you tell her?"

His daughter paused as if waiting for an audible answer. Josh worked to blink back his tears. Would any of this ever get easier? Ever?

"*Dat?*" Now it was David.

"What is it, son?"

"Do I gotta tell *Gott*, too?"

Cornelia huffed. "Course you don't. He knows you're my brother."

"He does know," Josh concurred.

"*Gut*," David mumbled and turned over to face the wall. Josh was quite certain he'd already fallen asleep, just that quickly.

Cornelia got up and threw her arms around Josh's waist. "I'm glad you're here still," she said, and then she crawled back into bed.

"So am I," Josh murmured. And in truth, he was glad, most of the time. And even when he wished he could avoid his life right then, he couldn't wish it for long. He had two beautiful children. And he never wanted to be ungrateful for them.

He kissed Cornelia's head. "*Gut* night," he whispered.

"*Gut* night," she whispered back.

He left their door open and went back downstairs to where his mother was waiting on the davenport in the front room. It was balmy that evening, so he left the front door open, but he did latch the screen door.

"Your *dat* built that screen door back when you were only knee-high," his mother said.

"I don't remember."

"You wouldn't," she went on. "Most everything you see around this old place, your *dat* built."

"I know."

"I wonder if he's building things in heaven."

Josh raised a brow. This was fanciful talk from his practical mother. He went to sit beside her. "How are you doing?" he asked gently.

She shook her head, and he saw her lower lip tremble slightly. "I'm fine. Question is, how are you?"

"I'm fine." He could play at this, too.

"I thought we might have waffles for breakfast. I remember Cornelia likes it when I mash up bananas into the batter."

"That she does."

His mother sighed. "Can you do the outside chores come morning?"

He frowned. "Of course, *Mamm*. I'll take care of everything outside."

"Except my flower beds," she said. "I don't want no one touching my beds."

He smiled, encouraged. Here was some of his mother's usual sass.

"How about the garden?" he asked playfully. She wouldn't want him messing with that, either.

She shrugged. "You can help me put it in. And help with the weeding when it's time."

He shot her a shocked glance. He was about to protest, asking her when she became so generous with her garden, but he stopped himself. She clearly wasn't strong enough to do it on her own, but her admitting it out loud showed him the depth of her depression. He'd never known her to admit she couldn't do something.

"All right," he said slowly. An awkward silence followed. He needed to tread lightly, and in truth, he wasn't sure how to do it. But something needed to be said about her watching the children.

She shifted her weight, as if she were uncomfortable.

"You need a pillow or something?" he asked.

"*Nee*, I don't need no pillow," she snapped.

"*Mamm?*"

"What?"

"I'm thinking about the *kinner*."

"What about them?"

"I'm thinking that I'd like to bring someone into the house to help. Adding two *kinner* and myself to the household is a lot for you." He held his breath.

His mother was studying him, and she didn't look any too pleased. "So..." she began, "you don't think I'm capable of minding your *kinner*? Have I gotten so old and useless as that?"

"*Mamm*," he protested. "I never said that."

She stood then, pulling her shoulders back. "*Jah*, you did. Now, I'm going to bed."

He watched her leave in stunned silence. So, they couldn't even talk about it? She wouldn't even entertain the notion? And goodness, it was only seven-thirty in the evening. Did she go to bed this early every night?

Not that he minded. But still, was she that tired?

He blew out his breath in huge sigh. He hadn't been there but a few hours, and he'd already offended her. How in the world was this going to work? But he knew one thing, they would need help. His mother wasn't capable of taking care of the increased household—he'd been naïve to think she would be. And Cornelia, though she was able to do quite a bit, wouldn't be able to help enough to make this work out well for all of them.

Besides, did he want to saddle his five-year-old with so much responsibility? And she'd be going to school in the fall.

No. They needed someone, whether his mother would admit it or not. He could go to the Feed & Supply tomorrow and talk to Eliza Troyer. The woman knew everything and everyone. She'd be able to suggest a helper for them.

Feeling better now he had a plan, Josh went out to the barn one more time, to make sure all was well for the night.

∼

Josh took Cornelia and David with him the next morning to the Feed & Supply. He didn't tell his mother what he planned to do. No need to get her upset again until he knew for sure he could get someone in. He thought it telling that Tamar didn't ask to come along with them that morning; she never used to pass up the chance to go into town. She especially loved chatting with Eliza and getting all the latest tidbits of news. In other words, gossip, though his mother would be the last to admit it.

He snapped the reins, and they took off down the drive.

"Can I have a piece of candy?" Cornelia asked, giving him her most impish smile.

He couldn't help but laugh. "*Ach*, Cornelia, what am I to do with you?"

"Give me a piece of candy?"

"I want one, too," David cried. He promptly stuck his two fingers in his mouth and started sucking.

"You can't have no candy cuz you're a *boppli*," Cornelia told him.

"I ain't neither a *boppli*," David said around his fingers.

"*Bopplis* suck their fingers. Big boys don't," Cornelia said matter-of-factly.

David pulled his fingers from his mouth with a scowl.

"You can both have one piece of nickel candy," Josh told them. "And then you can brush your teeth extra hard before bed."

They both grinned at that, well pleased. If only he could please his mother so easily. Or himself, for that matter. *Ach, Sara, I miss you so much.* He quickly sniffed away the tears that always threatened. Goodness, but a grown man shouldn't be so weak, should he? He set his jaw and concentrated on driving. Mercifully, Cornelia seemed content to watch the passing scenery, and David had gone back to sucking his fingers.

It wasn't long before they pulled into the expansive parking lot at the Feed & Supply. He secured the reins, climbed out, and helped both Cornelia and David down from the wagon. It was such a beautiful day that he hadn't hitched the covered buggy, instead wanting to be out in the air.

The children tore ahead of him into the store. He ambled in behind them.

"*Ach*, do my eyes deceive me? Is that you, Josh Lambright?" Eliza Troyer greeted him. "And don't tell me ... are these two your *kinner*?"

"Hello, Eliza," Josh said with a smile. "And *jah*. This here is my Cornelia and David."

"They're growing faster than newly planted corn," she said with a grin. "Now, how's your *mammi* doin', *kinner*?"

"She's right *gut*," Cornelia announced. "And she let me help make waffles."

Eliza feigned shock. "Did she now? My, but you must be a *gut* cook for her to let you help."

Cornelia nodded. "I been cookin' a lot."

"I don't suppose you two would be interested in a piece of nickel candy, now, would you?"

"*Jah*," David cried. "*Dat* said we could have one."

"How about if I let you each choose one?" Eliza said.

"*Jah*," David cried again.

Eliza picked up a huge glass pickle jar that had been repurposed as a candy jar. She came out from behind her counter and held it low for them to each choose a piece. Cornelia picked a round grape candy and David took a butterscotch.

"What do you say, *kinner*?" Josh asked.

"Thank you," they both said as they quickly unwrapped their pieces and popped them into their mouths.

Eliza straightened up and set the jar on the counter. "Now, what can I do for you, Josh?"

"I'm looking to get someone in to help *Mamm* with the cooking and the chores now we're here," he said. "Someone who wouldn't mind looking after the *kinner* some, too."

Eliza looked only mildly surprised. "Your *mamm* seems peaked these days. Your *dat's* passing hit her hard."

"That it did," he said, not mentioning how he hadn't realized just how hard until the day before.

"But now you're here, so things will look up for her."

"That's what I'm praying."

"And I was right sorry to hear of your loss, too, Josh. Right sorry."

"Thank you," he said, not wanting to talk about it. Mercifully, Eliza went back to the subject at hand.

"So, would this person be a live-in or do you just want someone during the day?"

Josh hadn't really considered live-in help, but there was no reason not to consider it. His mother had plenty of spare bedrooms in her old house.

"Could be either way," Josh said.

"Your *mamm* have any suggestions or names?"

He gave Eliza a sheepish look.

"Ahh," she said. "I see. She don't know yet. All right, Josh. I'll sniff around. It shouldn't be hard to find someone. Especially if you will take a teen girl."

Josh considered that for a moment. "I s'pose it'd be all right to have a teen, but I'd rather have someone a bit older. I think *Mamm* would like that better."

"All right," Eliza said, nodding. "Someone older."

Eliza looked over and smiled at Cornelia and David who were standing before a pile of apples looking at them.

Josh followed her gaze. "I think I'm going to have to buy two apples," he said with a grin.

"That you are," Eliza agreed.

# Chapter Four

Lucy finished sweeping the porch and took the broom back inside to the washroom. She'd saved her favorite chore until last—working the soil, preparing for the garden planting. She'd already put in the carrots and radishes and peas, as they would withstand any late frost. But she felt certain the frosts were over, at least, she hoped they were. Now, she could go on to plant tomatoes and peppers and eggplant. She had some herbs she wanted to grow that summer, too. If the weather turned cold again, she could cover them at night.

She pulled on her boots and headed out through the side door. She hadn't gotten far when her father's voice stopped her.

"Lucy!" Bartholomew's voice cracked.

She tensed and turned around.

"Where are you going?"

"Just out to the garden, *Dat*."

"What for? I don't smell no bread baking."

Lucy frowned. "What? What do you mean?"

"I mean, ain't it Tuesday? You bake bread on Tuesday. I don't want to be eatin' none of that store-bought bread. It ain't worthy of a slab of butter."

Lucy held her tongue. Not once in the last two years had she bought bread from the store. She'd made that mistake only one time. Once. She'd been super busy that week for it was canning time. She simply hadn't made the time to bake bread, thinking store-bought bread wouldn't be so bad. She'd been wrong. According to her dad, she'd committed some grave sin by purchasing bread.

He'd held up the plastic bag with the loaf sagging inside and shook it. "This ain't fit for man to eat."

"Sorry, *Dat*. Next time, I'll—"

He'd thrown the bread at her. "Get rid of it, and make me some decent bread," he'd snapped. "Don't ever waste my money like this again."

Lucy had bent over and gathered up the pieces of bread that had come out of the bag when he'd thrown it. Tears stung her eyes. She tried so hard to please her father. She'd been trying hard since her mother had died. But she never could please him. Never. Whatever she did was never enough. At that moment, she'd been exhausted, trying to do all the canning alone for the winter. She had stood over steaming pots all day long, after peeling and cutting and chopping.

It was then, after he'd thrown the bread at her that something inside her withered and died. She would never make her father happy, and she was tired of trying. Since that happened, she'd continued with all the work to be done, but now, she simply tried to avoid her father whenever she could.

At first, he didn't notice, but eventually, he did. And then he seemed bent on making her be around him whenever he was in the house. She hated it, but she put up with it—rebelling in her own quiet way. She didn't talk to him unless she had to. She didn't look at him unless she had to. She certainly didn't share any of her life with him.

But what was there to share? In truth, not much. Simply work. That was all she did. She'd long ago given up going to the youth singings. She wasn't interested in being courted, that was for sure and for certain. Her dreams were of a different nature entirely. She dreamed of being free. She dreamed of living on her own, making her own living, being self-sufficient.

She dreamed of having peace. No one to answer to. No one to serve.

It wasn't the normal Amish girl's dream; she knew that. But how she longed for it.

"Well?" her father snapped, bringing Lucy back to the present.

"I'll get to the bread this afternoon," she said, preparing to walk away.

"This afternoon?" he cried. "Your *mamm* always made bread in the morning. My *mamm* always made bread in the morning. You usually do. Now get in there and make it. It needs to rise, don't it?"

Five years. Five years, she'd been taking care of everything. She certainly knew that bread needed to rise.

She looked at his flushed face and knew this conversation had nothing to do with bread. He was in a mood, and he wanted to control her.

She could argue with him, but it wouldn't go well. She had suffered more than one bruise when she had taken that course.

So, she nodded. "*Jah, Dat*. It has to rise. I'll go make it now."

He sputtered a bit, as though he hadn't expected her to agree so readily. She brushed past him, cringing as her elbow accidentally touched his arm. She went into the washroom and kicked off her boots. Then she picked them up and put them neatly beneath the bench. She walked into the kitchen and took out a large glass bowl. She set it on the counter and stared at it, her eyes welling with tears.

How much longer could she put up with this? Her father could live for decades yet. She sucked in her breath. Was she wishing for his death? *Ach,* but she was a wicked woman. But it was true, and she couldn't shake it. She wished her father was no longer here. The depth of her yearning was so startling she sank down on a kitchen bench.

She needed to leave. Somehow, some way, she needed to leave. She couldn't go on like this. She didn't even recognize herself anymore. She rarely even smiled anymore.

She had to get out of here.

*Dear Gott, please provide me a way out. Please.*

# Chapter Five

The day passed quickly as Josh got everything in order to begin planting a crop of soybeans. If all went well, he should have the seeds in the ground by the end of next week. Still timely enough to have a good crop, if God willed it.

He'd left the children in his mother's care for the day, having no other option—yet. But he was hopeful Eliza Troyer would come up with a suggestion right soon. He needed to talk with his mother about it again, and that was going to happen tonight. It had to, for as soon as he had a name, he was going to try and get the woman to start immediately.

He rubbed his forearm over his brow, wiping the sweat onto his sleeve. It had been a good day. He'd worked hard and had felt a sense of purpose. It had taken his mind off things, too, which was a welcome relief.

He surveyed all his father's tools, now freshly organized. He'd done enough for the day. He tossed his work gloves onto the work bench and headed for the house. He went through the side door into the washroom and took off his shoes. He then washed up. He heard his children hollering from the front room and wondered what in the world they were fussing about this time.

He strode through the kitchen—which was strangely empty, for he'd expected to see his mother making supper—and went into the front room. Cornelia saw him and rushed to him.

"*Dat*, David keeps wrecking everything I build," she cried, pointing to a jumble of wooden blocks splayed across the braided rug.

"*Nee*, I don't," David countered.

"*Jah*, you do!"

"Enough," Josh said sternly. "It ain't *gut* to fight. You should be getting along. Now, I'm sure there are enough blocks for both of you to have plenty. Cornelia, you divide them up, will you?"

She scowled but sat down to begin dividing the blocks into two piles. Josh glanced around for his mother.

"Where's your *mammi*?" he asked.

"She said we was giving her a headache," David volunteered, sticking his two fingers in his mouth to begin sucking.

"That's no surprise, now, is it?" he asked. He left them and went upstairs. He knocked gently on his mother's bedroom door, which was ajar. He poked his head in and she jumped up from the bed.

"*Ach*, I didn't hear you come in."

"No reason to. I'm just checking on you."

"I-I'm fine. Why wouldn't I be? I just came up here to... I just came up to fetch a fresh *kapp*." She hurried to the dresser and began to fumble inside the top drawer.

"*Mamm*..." he said.

"What?" She put on a smile. "I'll have supper in a jiffy."

Her bustling about, pretending she was fine, had worn her out. He could hear her breath puffing and her face was pale.

"Sit down, *Mamm*," he said, pointing to the bed.

She pressed her lips into a tight line but did as she was told. He sat beside her.

"I know us coming is a lot," he said. "It wasn't my intent to see you take on too much—"

"It ain't too much," she interrupted him, her voice fierce.

"*Mamm*, please. It's a lot. And I want to bring in someone to help."

"I don't need help in my own house," she said defiantly.

"Fine. But *I* need help with my *kinner*," he said. "They're a handful, and I know it."

"I can take care of the *kinner*," she insisted.

Josh sighed. "*Jah, Mamm*, I'm sure you can. But I won't feel right about it. So I guess I'm bringing someone in for me."

"That's a waste of money. Who knows what it'll cost you?" She shook her head. "Too much. I can do it for nothing."

"I don't want you doing it for nothing, *Mamm*. It's too late, anyway. I've already spoken with Eliza Troyer, and she's going to help me find someone."

His mother sucked in a loud breath. "You've gone behind my back to ask around?" she cried. "And to Eliza? *Ach*, now she'll think I can't take care of my own family."

"*Mamm*, stop. Eliza won't think any such thing." But he knew differently. Of course, she would. He knew how women folk looked at things. His Sara had taught him quite a little. Nevertheless, it didn't change the facts. His mother needed help.

Tamar shook her head over and over. "I don't like it."

Josh sighed. "You don't have to like it. But please, just let me do this. I want to. And later, if it doesn't work out well, we can talk about it again."

His mother perked up at that. "So, if it don't work out, you'll let her go?"

His brow furrowed. He didn't like his mother's tone—would she purposely sabotage this?

"I said we can talk about it again."

His mother gave a soft snort. "Fine. I guess you've already done it anyhow."

He leaned over and gave his mother a peck on the cheek—something he rarely did. "Thank you, *Mamm*."

⁓

"I'm just telling you what I heard," Greta Byler said.

Lucy looked at her cousin. "You're sure. In Hollybrook?"

"*Jah*. It ain't so far away."

Lucy didn't care how far away it was. In truth, the further, the better, but she certainly wasn't going to tell Greta that.

"You told me you was looking for a job." Greta shrugged. "I don't reckon this one will work out any too well. Your *dat* wouldn't be wanting you so far away from him. I know he counts on you."

Lucy bit her tongue. Greta didn't know the half of it. But now, her mind was soaring with the possibility of a job in Hollybrook.

"And it's a live-in job?"

Greta frowned. "You already asked. *Jah*, it's a live-in job. You'd be caring for two young *kinner* and helping with the household chores. I'm not sure about the wife... Maybe she's ill. I don't know. But the *mammi* lives there, too, so it would be all proper-like."

"So, what do I have to do?"

"I don't know. But I do know it's the Lambrights. Not sure how many Lambrights in Hollybrook, but there can't be that many."

Lucy raised a brow.

Greta laughed. "All right, there could be a whole passel of them. But if you stop at the mercantile, they'll know."

"I'd have to actually go there then?"

"There might be a phone shanty close, but I never heard that. And I wouldn't have the number anyway."

"But what if I go all that way, and they already have someone?"

Greta shrugged. "A wasted trip, I guess."

But if Lucy didn't go, she for sure wouldn't get the job. And she wanted it. She wanted it more than she'd ever wanted anything in her life. Her father would be furious, but so be it. She was twenty-seven years old—plenty old enough to leave home. But she'd have to go without him knowing what she was doing, for he surely would forbid it.

"You could take the bus," Greta suggested. "It wouldn't cost very much, and you'd be there right quick."

Lucy nodded, already planning it out. "Will you go with me?" she asked.

Greta considered. "I s'pose I could."

If Lucy could tell her father she would be with Greta, he'd be more inclined to allow her to be gone. He liked his niece, which confounded Lucy, for as far as she could tell, he didn't like anyone.

"Thank you. Is tomorrow too soon?" Lucy had a sudden fear that if she didn't move quickly, she would miss her chance. And she simply couldn't miss it—this position seemed like a gift from God.

Greta laughed. "You're eager. I didn't think you'd go for it since you'd have to live there. I don't think *Onkel* is going to like it."

Lucy swallowed. "Let's not tell him until I know for sure, all right? No reason to worry him."

Greta looked hesitant, but she finally agreed. "I think the bus leaves at nine o'clock. At least, it used to. I'll have Abner drive us there in the buggy. We'll come by around—"

"*Nee*," Lucy said quickly, cutting her off. "Don't come by. I'll ride my bicycle to your house."

"But you don't ne—"

"I want to." Lucy stood up "See you tomorrow, then?"

Greta looked surprised at being clearly dismissed. "All right. See you tomorrow."

Lucy's heart was racing. She needed Greta to leave before her father showed up and Greta let something slip. She walked to the edge of the porch and gazed about for signs of her father, but she didn't see him. He was likely in the fields. She'd tell him at supper she'd be going somewhere the next day.

*Ach*, her green dress was in the laundry, and it was her prettiest dress. The rich color was like evergreen needles. Well, she'd have to wear her dark purple dress; she didn't like it as much, but it'd have to do.

She went inside to fix a hearty supper for her father. She'd tell him after he'd eaten that she was spending the day with Greta. She prayed he'd be agreeable, because agreeable or not, she was going.

∾

Three hours later, Bartholomew scooted back from the table and belched. Lucy caught herself before grimacing. She hated it when her father displayed such bad manners, but she'd learned a long time ago not to say anything. Now, she put on a smile.

"Did you like the roast beef sandwich?"

His eyes narrowed. "You wanting a compliment for doing your work?"

"*Nee, nee.* I just hoped you liked supper."

He tipped his head to the side. "It was passable."

She kept her smile in place. "*Dat,* tomorrow Greta wants me to spend some time with her—"

"Didn't I see her buggy here this afternoon?"

Lucy nodded. "*Jah,* and we thought it would be fun to work together tomorrow on some ... quilting." She was downright lying now, but she didn't know what else to do.

"Quilting?" He smiled. "That Greta. She is quite the quilter, *ain't so?*"

"*Jah,*" Lucy agreed, smiling wider. "She's quite skilled at it."

"She's *gut* at a lot of things." He folded his hand across his belly beneath his beard. "I s'pose spending some time over there wouldn't hurt." He looked at her, his expression hardening. "Don't ignore your own chores, daughter. And leave me my meal in the refrigerator."

"I will, *Dat,* don't worry." Lucy's heart lifted. This had been much easier than she'd feared.

"I ain't worryin'," he said. He stood and scooted his chair under the table. "I'll be wanting some iced tea in the front room."

And with that, he turned and left.

"Of course, *Dat*," she said, still smiling.

# Chapter Six

Lucy tried not to be vain. She rarely checked her appearance in the hand-held mirror she kept atop her dresser. But this day, this day, she checked herself repeatedly. She simply had to make a good impression on the Lambrights. She twisted her hair into a tight bun three times until she was satisfied. She put on two different *kapps*, finally deciding the second one was a bit crisper. She yearned for a full-length mirror so she could check her dress from all angles.

Finally in exasperation, she left her room and went downstairs. She'd already fixed her father's meals for the day, placing them in the refrigerator where they couldn't be missed. She glanced around the house to make sure all was tidy. Satisfied, she hurried out to the barn to get on her bicycle. Her *dat* was already out in the fields, so she didn't say good-bye. Just as well, for this way, he couldn't come up with an excuse for her not to go.

She jumped on her bike and rode quickly off the property and onto the road. Greta's house was about a mile away, so it wouldn't take long at all to get there. When she rode up the driveway, she saw Greta waiting for her.

"Hello," Lucy called out.

Greta rushed down the front steps to meet her. "I can't go," she said.

Lucy gaped at her. "What?"

"I can't go. *Mamm* made arrangements for me to babysit Raymond's *kinner*."

"Surely your brother can find someone else."

Greta shrugged. "It's too late. *Mamm* agreed for me. I have to do it."

"But—"

Greta held up her hand. "Don't worry. Abner will still drive you to the station. He's in the barn with the goats."

"But—"

"I'm so sorry, Lucy. But I can't help it. You'll be fine on your own."

Lucy's mind whirled. What if her father ran into Greta somehow? He'd know Lucy had lied. But then, it hadn't been a lie when she'd told him.

But it had. She wasn't going to be quilting at all.

"Don't look so worried," Greta told her. "Here's Abner now."

Lucy turned to see Abner leading the buggy horse out of the barn. He took her straight to the buggy at the side of the barn and began hitching her up. He glanced up and saw her and waved.

"I can have him pick you up, too. I reckon you'll come back on the afternoon bus."

Lucy nodded, assuming that was what would happen. She felt completely ferhoodled right then. But Greta was right. She could do this alone. Goodness, she was a grown woman.

"I'll be thinking of you," Greta told her. "And *Gott's* blessing on you."

Lucy leaned her bike against the porch railing, gave Greta a wobbly smile, and went to get into the buggy. She settled into the front seat and Abner got in.

"Thank you for taking me," Lucy said.

"Ah, won't take me long. What are you going to Hollybrook for, anyway?"

Lucy hesitated. She had no wish to tell Abner where she was going or that it was a secret. What excuse could she possibly give him?

He studied her. "You do have a reason, don't you?"

"*Jah, jah*," she said with a laugh. "I was just thinking of something else. I want to pick up a few things there. You know they have more selection that we do here. Fabric. That's what I'm looking for. I'm going to make a new dress."

*Ach*, the lies kept growing. Unless she did buy a measure of fabric. She mentally went through the money in her purse. She might have enough to buy fabric for a new dress.

"You got a *gut* dress right there," he said, nodding at her dress. "Don't see why you women need more than one or two dresses."

She scoffed. "Abner Byler, I hope you ain't courting anyone. No girl is going to want a husband who thinks like that."

He laughed right out at that. "I'll keep that in mind, cousin."

"You do that."

Still chuckling, he snapped the reins on the horse's rear end and the buggy sped up a bit. They made it to the wide spot in the road where the bus stopped.

"I'll leave you here," he said, "if that's all right. Bus should be coming along any minute."

"That's fine. Thanks, Abner."

"I'll be back to get you this afternoon. If I ain't here, start walking and I'll meet you soon enough."

"All right. Bye now."

She climbed out of the buggy and joined two other people who were clearly waiting for the bus, too. *Englischers,* they were. They nodded their greeting, and she nodded back. Within minutes, the bus came to a loud grinding halt in front of them. She climbed on and paid the driver for a ticket to Hollybrook. She found an empty seat and settled in.

When the bus started down the road, she closed her eyes, willing herself to relax. Everything was going to be fine. If this position was for her, God would pave the way.

*Please, Gott, let this be for me. Let me move out of my house and start a new life in Hollybrook. Please.*

She was too restless to relax. She opened her eyes and entertained herself by making up stories about the other passengers. One lady sitting in the next seat up across the aisle was wearing a large straw hat with fake sunflowers. Lucy made up an entire life story for her: She was visiting her long-lost grandchildren who would recognize her by the hat. She'd been in a foreign country for years as a missionary and had only just come back. She was going to move in with her daughter, although her daughter wasn't completely welcoming. She was—

Lucy stopped herself. Why had she turned the story negative?

*Because your* dat *has never been welcoming to you...*

She shivered. If he knew where she was at this very moment and what she was intending to do, he would hit her. She jerked. Hit her? Why had she thought that? He had hit her in the past, it was true... But why would her mind go there so quickly?

She clenched her jaw. If her mind was going these places, it truly meant she needed to leave. *Ach*, but her mother would be heartbroken if she knew. Did she know? Could she see them from heaven? Most times, Lucy wished her mother could see her, but not right then. There was no need for her mother to know.

By the time the bus pulled into the stop at Hollybrook, Lucy was exhausted. And so weary of her own thoughts. She stepped down from the bus and looked around. She knew Hollybrook only vaguely, but she did remember that the local mercantile, the Feed & Supply, was fairly close to the bus stop. The day was beautiful; clear, and sunny, so walking there should be no problem.

She set out, focusing on the sound of the breeze through the trees and the sight of the spring flowers already popping up in fragrant clumps. Hollybrook was a nice place; she wouldn't mind living there at all. Before an hour had passed, she was walking into the Feed & Supply, ushered in with the sound of the tinkling bell above the door.

"*Gut* morning," said the stout woman behind the counter. "Might I be helping you?"

"Hello," Lucy said, approaching her. "I'm looking for the Lambright place."

"*Ach*," the woman cried. "I'm Eliza Troyer. Welcome. You must be here for the helper position."

Lucy's brow rose in surprise. "I am."

"*Gut*. Where are you from? I know everyone around here."

"I'm from Marksville down the way."

"So you took the bus?" Eliza craned around to peer through the outside window. "Or did you hire a van?"

"I took the bus."

"So you're walking?"

Lucy nodded. "Are the Lambrights close?"

Eliza frowned. "Well, they ain't too far, but you've already walked quite a spell." She walked out from behind the counter. "Jason King is here getting some supplies for his *mamm*. I'll ask him to take you."

"*Ach, nee*. I couldn't be bothering him."

Eliza swished her hand through the air. "It won't be no trouble. Jason?" she called out.

A young teen appeared from the end of an aisle. His straw hat was slightly askew, and his blond hair stuck out from under the brim. "*Jah*, Eliza?"

"Can you be taking..." she paused and looked at Lucy. "What's your name?"

"I'm Lucy Oyer."

"Can you take Lucy Oyer to the Lambrights on your way home?"

He shrugged. "I can."

"*Gut.* It's settled then." She looked again at Lucy. "You thirsty? I have some cartons of juice in the cooler."

"*Nee,* I'm fine. Truly. But thank you."

"I'm sure you're thirsty even if you don't think you are." She walked to the cooler and reached in, taking out a carton of orange juice. Here you are." She handed Lucy the drink.

Lucy took it and then laid her bag on the counter. She dug inside with her free hand to find her change purse.

"*Nee,* you don't owe me a penny. You just drink it and refresh yourself." Eliza tilted her head slightly, studying Lucy. "Now, tell me about yourself."

Lucy blinked. "There ain't much to tell. I'm from Marksville—"

"*Jah*, I know that. You got siblings? How about your folks? Does your family farm? Or are they factory folks?"

Lucy's eyes widened, and then she understood: Eliza was the woman who knew every tidbit of information and gossip in the district. She was merely doing what she did best: pry. Lucy smiled, relaxing. There was an Eliza in every Amish district.

"I don't have siblings," she said. "My *mamm* died five years ago—"

"*Ach*, I'm so sorry," Eliza tsk-ed.

"And my *dat* does farm."

"So, your *dat* will be joining you here in Hollybrook if you take the position. Take up a farm here?"

Lucy's heart raced. "*Nee*. He needs to stay on his farm."

"He can't be too happy to lose you, then." She frowned. "Or maybe he's sweet on someone."

Lucy couldn't imagine her father sweet on anyone, but she couldn't say that, so she merely shrugged.

Eliza chuckled. "I imagine he is, then."

Just then, Jason approached the counter with his basket full of items.

"I'll get these put on your account right quick," Eliza told him, returning to her post behind the counter. She finished up and bagged Jason's goods.

*1*

"Shall we go?" Jason asked Lucy.

"*Jah*, thank you," Lucy said, hurrying to match his stride as he left the store. She turned around and gave Eliza a quick wave of thanks before walking out the door.

Jason had brought a pony cart with him, so Eliza sat in the back on an overturned apple box. It was fine with her. She was becoming nervous, and she didn't want to have to converse. All she could do was think about what the Lambrights might be like. And what about the *kinner*? Would they take to her? She hoped they would and right away, too. She wanted this job so badly, the mere thought of not getting it was painful.

"Here we are," Jason said later as he pulled up to a very traditional white farmhouse. The flower beds hadn't been seen to, but Lucy would enjoy working on those. The *kinner* could help her. It would be fun.

"Thank you," Lucy said, climbing out of the back of the cart.

"Welcome," he said, snapping the reins and heading out.

# Chapter Seven

Lucy stood there, facing the porch of the house. She swallowed with difficulty and then climbed the porch steps. The front door was open, so she knocked on the rim of the screen door.

"I'll get it," she heard a child holler. Within seconds, a young girl came to the door. "Hello," she said, staring at Lucy.

"Hello," Lucy said. "What's your name?"

"I'm Cornelia. I wish I had a nickname, but I don't wanna be called Corn." She giggled. "Whoever heard of someone called Corn?"

"*Nee*, Corn won't do at all. How about Nellie?"

Cornelia scratched her head. "Nellie?" She bit her lip as if contemplating something of extreme importance. Then she laughed. "*Jah!* I like Nellie."

"Nellie, is your *dat* here?"

Cornelia pushed through the screen door to join her on the porch and gazed toward the barn. "I dunno. I s'pose he's in the barn or something."

Lucy was quite sure he wasn't in the barn, or he would have heard the pony cart and come out to greet it.

"Is your *mamm* or *mammi* here?" Lucy asked. "You live with your *mammi, ain't so?*"

Cornelia nodded.

Just then an even younger boy came running to the door. "Who are you?" he asked.

"I'm Lucy," she said at the same moment Cornelia said, "She's my friend."

Lucy smiled at the girl. "Thank you. I want to be friends."

"She ain't my friend," the boy said.

"Ah, David, that's cuz you don't know her yet," Cornelia said. "She's nice. She gave me my new name."

"Huh?" David's face screwed up into a question mark.

"You can call me Nellie now."

"Huh? Nellie?"

Cornelia nodded proudly. "I'm Nellie. I need to go tell *Mammi*. You can come inside."

"You ain't Nellie," David said, following her as she disappeared back into the house.

Lucy smiled and stepped just inside the door. She already liked both of the children, especially Cornelia. There was just something about the girl's spirit that sparked admiration in Lucy. She hoped she would get to spend a lot of time with the girl. David, too, she thought.

Within minutes, a frail-looking woman with nearly sold gray hair tucked severely under her *kapp* came toward the door.

"Can I help you?" she asked.

"Hello, I'm Lucy Oyer. I'm here about the helper position."

The woman's expression soured, and Lucy had a moment of panic, wondering what was wrong. Was something the matter with her appearance? Had they already filled the job? Was there something on her face?

"What's a helper position?" Cornelia asked, tugging on the woman's apron.

"Never you mind," said the woman. Her voice sounded defeated, and Lucy got a strange feeling in her stomach. Something was amiss. Her spirits fell—was this not going to work out after all? And where was the mother? Her opinion would likely have more sway that the grandmother's.

"Have I come at a bad moment?" Lucy asked. "You didn't know I was coming. I'm sorry. I would have phoned, but I didn't have the number of the nearest shanty. I just—"

The older woman held up her hand. "Please," she said, stopping Lucy's flood of words. "It's my son you need to be talking to."

Lucy took a deep breath. "Ah. Okay." Hope sprang again. Maybe this would be all right after all.

She waited for the woman to direct her to her son, but she didn't. She merely stood there and looked at her. Finally, Lucy said, "Where can I find your son?"

"Outside," David said.

"Thank you, David. I'll go on out and see if I can find him."

"I'm comin', too," Cornelia said.

"Me, too," David added.

"That's fine," Lucy told them and the three of them went back out through the screen door. The children raced ahead straight to the fields. Lucy immediately saw a figure at the north end of the field. Cornelia was already hollering at him, waving her hands as her feet padded over the newly planted fields. Lucy cringed, hoping she wasn't ruining any of the seeds. David was keeping up right well, too, as he flew behind Cornelia.

Their father stopped and turned toward them. He waved back and picked his way through the field to join them. Hesitantly, Lucy stayed put, unsure whether to tromp out there to meet him or not. She decided to wait as they were all headed her way.

"This is her," Cornelia said. "She calls me Nellie."

"Is that so?" the man said. He brushed a wisp of brown hair from his sweaty forehead and stopped before her. His brown eyes were deep and warm and curious.

"I-I'm Lucy. Lucy Oyer," she began, clearing her throat. "I heard you're looking for someone to watch the *kinner* and help with the housework."

"Did you talk to Eliza?" he asked.

"Eliza? At the Feed & Supply? *Jah*, she told me where to find you."

"So you live around here?"

"*Nee?* I'm from Marksville."

He looked puzzled. "You heard about the job in Marksville?"

"My cousin told me about it."

"So you came by bus? Or hired van?"

"Bus."

He rubbed his hands down his thighs. "*Ach*, let me introduce myself. I'm Josh Lambright. Just moved back home here recently. These are my *kinner*, Cornelia and David."

"*Dat*, I'm Nellie now," Cornelia said.

Josh laughed. "Are you now?"

"*Jah*, it's my nickname."

"I see."

"I hope you don't mind," Lucy said. "We were chatting, and she wanted a nickname."

"Nellie sounds fine." He reached over and gave Cornelia's shoulder a squeeze. "This job is a live-in job." He looked at her frankly. "Would that suit?"

Her heart was hammering. Now that she'd met the father, she was even more interested. He seemed kind, and, well, *normal*. Unlike her father. She wouldn't have to walk about waiting for him to explode.

"It would suit," she said quickly. She tried to temper herself; she didn't want to look too eager.

"It seems you've already made friends with the *kinner*. Let's go meet my *mamm*."

"She already did," Cornelia piped up. "*Mammi* talked to her already."

A look of concern flashed across his face but was immediately gone again. Lucy wondered at that. For it was certainly true that his mother hadn't been welcoming. Something was going on. Lucy bit her lip. Was she willing to come share a home with a woman who didn't want her? Wouldn't that be as bad as living with her father?

No. It wouldn't. Surely not.

"My *mamm* ain't too keen on getting in help," Josh told her. He looked down at his children. "You two run off now and tell *Mammi* we'd like some iced tea. Can you do that? Run along, now."

Cornelia and David took off around the house.

"My *dat* has recently passed, and *Mamm*, well, she is still grieving."

"Of course," Lucy murmured, her heart going out to the woman. Lucy wanted to know what had happened to the children's mother. Something had to have happened. Perhaps, she was upstairs and ill. "And... your wife?"

He blinked. "She... We lost her five months ago." He hesitated and then went on, "She had an accident. Fell from the barn loft. The *kinner*... Well, we moved here and are starting over."

"I'm so sorry," Lucy said. And she was. What a horrible thing to happen. And the poor children, what a devastating blow. But while she was truly sorry for what had happened, she also felt relief. If the man was a recent widower, she wouldn't have to be concerned about anything occurring between them. Not that she wanted to be presumptuous, but she had no wish whatever to become close to him, and now she knew he would feel the same.

This position was truly a gift from God.

"*Mamm* is struggling," he told her, his voice low. "But she doesn't like to admit it. I didn't know when we moved here that she was ... weaker. But when I realized, I suggested we get someone in to help. You've met my Cornelia." He paused to smile fondly. "She's a handful. Anyway, *Mamm* isn't in favor, but I insisted. She's really a lovely woman, friendly and welcoming. But you might have to give her some time to adjust."

"It's fine," Lucy said. "She seems right nice."

She felt like jumping for joy. The way he was talking, she had the job.

He started walking then, heading for the house. She scurried to keep up with his long stride. When they headed inside, they heard Cornelia chattering away from another room. David was in the front room, playing with wooden blocks.

"Are you building a tower?" Lucy asked.

He carefully balanced another block onto the six stacked blocks. He didn't look at her, but he did nod. She got down on the rug with him.

"Can I help?"

He seemed to consider this quite seriously before he nodded again. She picked up a block. "Shall I?"

"*Jah.*"

She placed the block on the stack. It teetered and she gave a playful gasp. But it stabilized, and David looked up at her with a big grin.

"You did it."

"So I did," she agreed. She glanced over at Josh who was watching them with a look of relief on his face.

Cornelia came rushing into the room. "We got the tea," she said, nearly hollering.

"Not so loud, daughter," Josh said.

*Mammi* came in carrying a tray of glasses filled with iced tea.

"This is my *mamm*, Tamar Lambright," Josh introduced her. "*Mamm*, this is Lucy Oyer."

"We met," the woman said, her lips tight.

Josh gave Lucy an apologetic look. "She's going to be helping the *kinner*," he said. He glanced again at Lucy. "Will you? I'm sorry. I didn't ask properly."

Lucy nodded.

"You mean, she's gonna stay with us?" Cornelia asked.

"That she is."

"*Gut*," Cornelia cried, going right over and plopping down beside Lucy on the rug.

"We need to discuss your wages, too," he said. He watched his mother hand out the glasses of tea. He appeared reluctant to discuss money in front of her, which Lucy understood. If the woman didn't even want her there, she'd consider Lucy's wages a huge waste of money.

"I'll need to go back to Marksville to gather my things before I can start," she said.

"Of course. I'll hire a van for you," Josh offered.

"There's no need. I can take the bus."

Josh shrugged. "If you like, but I'll pay for the ticket."

"You live in Marksville?" Tamar asked. "I didn't think I recognized you from around here."

"*Jah*. But I'm glad to be moving to Hollybrook," she said, smiling.

"Why? You trying to get out of Marksville? You don't like it?"

Lucy flinched. Goodness, but the woman was harsh. "I... I..."

"*Mamm*," Josh interceded. "I'm sure Lucy likes Marksville right fine. But the job is here."

Tamar's mouth tightened, but she didn't say anything further.

Lucy stayed a bit longer to play with the children, but not long. She was eager to get back to Marksville now and get packed. She ignored completely the thought of telling her father; though, she knew she'd have to.

"I don't think the bus leaves for a few hours yet," Josh told her. "You can stay if you like."

"*Nee*, I'll get back to the bus stop. Maybe there's an earlier bus."

"There could be. I don't really know. Don't have much occasion to think about Marksville."

He wouldn't, as Hollybrook was larger and had more of everything.

"I'll hitch up the pony cart and take you in."

"Thank you," Lucy told him. She was still a bit overcome to have gotten the job so easily. He hadn't questioned her at all, which she had expected. She wondered why he agreed to her with no further information. Or had he already exhausted the possibilities locally. That seemed hardly likely, either.

When he had the cart hitched, she bid the children farewell. She wanted to say good-bye to Tamar also, but the woman seemed to have disappeared. She went outside and got into the cart. Josh's cart was bigger than Jason's, the teen who had delivered her there. Josh's cart had enough space to fit two on the driver's bench, so that was where she sat.

"Can I go?" Cornelia asked, having followed Lucy outside.

"Not today, daughter," Josh told her. "Go on in and help *Mammi* wash up the tea glasses."

Cornelia made an exaggerated face of disgust, but she followed her father's prompting. Lucy was sorry she hadn't tagged along, for she didn't relish being alone with Josh and having to think of something to say. But as soon as they took off down the road, she surprised herself by asking, "Why did you hire me so quick-like? You don't know a thing about me."

Josh's brow rose, and he turned to give her a brief glance before focusing on the road ahead. "Because I just knew."

She studied his profile, appreciating the strength of his jawline and the strong slope of his nose. "Knew?" she questioned.

"I prayed about it and asked *Gott* to let me know who would be best to watch the *kinner*. And who would be best to get along with *Mamm*. I knew she was going to be a ... well, a hardship. At first, at least. When I saw you, it was as if *Gott* told me, 'It's her.'"

He looked at her again, frankly, his expression matter-of-fact.

"Oh," she murmured, not having anything more to add. If he thought God had answered his prayer with her, then who was she to argue? Besides, she didn't want to argue at all. She was beyond pleased to have the job. She already felt a burning sense of purpose and fulfillment simply thinking about helping to raise the two *kinner*. And Tamar? If Lucy could get along with her father, then she surely could get along with Tamar.

Beside her, Josh chuckled. "You see what I mean?"

She frowned in confusion.

"You don't seem a bit put off by my *mamm*. Another reason I know you're the right person for the job."

She smiled then.

"Can I ask you something?" he said.

"What is it?" She shifted uncomfortably. Something told her she wasn't going to like his questions. And she was right. She didn't.

"Can I ask why you don't have a family of your own? *Kinner* and a husband."

She must have given him an affronted look, for he quickly backtracked.

"*Ach*, sorry. I can see I've overstepped."

She nodded. "You have."

He looked a bit slighted by her cold response, but he didn't comment further. In truth, he didn't say another word before arriving at the bus stop. Lucy was regretting her brusqueness by then. Was she jeopardizing her job before she even got started? But no, for when he pulled his horse to a stop, he turned to her and said, "We need to discuss your wages. You likely need to know what they are before committing completely to the job."

He went on to outline her pay, the hours he expected, and her days off. It was all acceptable. In truth, more than acceptable. What she didn't tell him was she would have worked for no wages in exchange for free room and board, she was so eager to get away from her father. But then, she did deserve a wage for she would be working and working hard.

"It all sounds right fine," she said, careful to smile and hopefully ease his impression of her.

"*Gut.* When do you think you can return?"

"Tomorrow."

"As soon as that?"

She nodded. She wanted to get away quickly once she told her father her plans. She feared if she had to stay much at all, he would find some way to stop her.

"All right. I'll pick you up tomorrow morning when the bus gets in."

She climbed down from the cart. "Thank you."

He gave her a small wave and turned the pony cart around easily with the wide shoulders on the road. She watched him leave and felt the first stirrings of panic. What had she *done?* She had to make a plan—figure out how she was going to tell her father she was leaving the next day. It was sudden, abrupt. And perhaps, thoughtless of her. But she had to get away. She known that for years. She couldn't start second-guessing herself now.

God had given her an out, and she was taking it.

As it turned out, there wasn't an earlier bus. She waited for hours at the side of the road. By the time the bus screeched to a halt before her, she was tired and dusty and not a little frantic. She could think of no way to tell her father but to just blurt it out. She climbed onto the bus, paid for her passage, and gratefully found most of the bus was empty. They'd be stopping along the way to pick up others, but it shouldn't fill up. She leaned back against the vinyl seat and closed her eyes. Maybe she could doze off. She'd like that as then she would stop thinking.

# Chapter Eight

"I don't like her," Tamar said over the supper table.

Josh sighed heavily and put down his fork. "Why not?"

"Who?" Cornelia asked. "Who don't you like?"

Josh gave his mother an accusatory look. "We shouldn't discuss this now anyway."

"Why not? The *kinner* aren't blind. That girl is no *gut*."

Josh was angry now. "How can you say that? And do you have so little faith in me? You think I'd turn over the care of my *kinner* to a person who ain't *gut*?"

Tamar shrugged. "Looks like you have."

"You mean Lucy?" Cornelia cried. "I like her, *Mammi*. She's nice."

Tamar reached over and rubbed Cornelia's back.

"So do I," David said, although he was carefully looking at his *mammi*. "I think. Maybe I don't."

"Of course, you like her," Josh stated, his voice perhaps a bit too loud. "We *all* like her. *Mammi* was confused."

Tamar looked irritated, but she didn't say a thing.

"How come you don't like her?" Cornelia asked. "She even gave me my new name."

Tamar grabbed hold of that comment. "See what I mean? Here she is for not more than ten seconds, and she's renaming your daughter. Who would do such a thing?"

"It's my nickname, *Mammi*. I'm still Cornelia."

Josh picked up his fork and speared a chunk of cooked carrot. "We ain't talking about this right now. Cornelia, did you feed the chickens today?"

"*Dat*," Cornelia said with exasperation. "You know I did. You helped me."

Josh laughed. "Goodness, am I forgetting so easily?" He laughed again, wanting to lighten the mood.

David started to laugh. "Member when I forgotted to brush my teeth?"

"You always forget to brush your teeth," Cornelia told him.

"*Nee*, I don't," David said. "Do I, *Dat*?"

"*Jah*, you do," Cornelia slipped the words in.

"*Nee*, you don't," Josh told him. "But sometimes, you do forget."

David nodded. "But not all the time."

"*Nee*, not all the time."

Cornelia took a big bite of mashed potatoes. "*Mammi*, these are so *gut*."

"Don't talk with your mouth full. It's bad manners," Tamar scolded her.

"Will Lucy eat with us?" Cornelia asked. "Will she got bad manners, too?"

Josh sighed. So, they were back around to Lucy again. Well, it couldn't go on like this for long. Lucy would move in and become such a help that his mother would forget all about being cold to her. Soon they would be close friends. He felt sure of it.

For hadn't God led Lucy to them in the first place?

∼

As good as his word, Abner was there to pick Lucy up when she got off the bus. He waved when she spotted him. She hurried over and climbed in the back of the pony cart, balancing once again on the overturned apple box.

"Did you get everything done?" he asked. He was clearly checking for her parcels, of which she had none.

"Mostly," she finally said. "Thank you for coming to fetch me."

"Weren't no bother," he said. "I'll just take you straight home. You can fetch your bicycle another day. Does that suit?"

No, it truly didn't suit. But she supposed it didn't matter much right now anymore. There was no need to keep anything secret. Her father was going to know the true score right quick.

"That's fine," she said.

They drove on in silence, which suited Lucy fine. By the time they reached her home, her heart was hammering. As Abner turned into the drive, she wanted to tell him to turn around and quickly. Of course, she didn't. When he let her off, she barely spoke a word to him, she was so distracted and nervous. Thank goodness, he was in too much of a hurry to want to stay and greet his uncle.

She did manage a wave and a thank you as he drove off.

She turned to face the house. This was it. And since she was leaving the next day, she needed to get it over with fast. She

# THE RECENT WIDOWER

climbed the steps and hadn't even gotten to the door, when her father pushed through the screen.

"About time you got back. Was that Abner? Why didn't he stop in for a minute?"

"I don't know."

"Now you can make me a hot meal instead of that cold one in the refrigerator."

"Fine." She brushed past him to go to the kitchen. He followed her. "So how is Greta? Her folks?"

"Everyone is fine." Her throat had gone dry. She tried to swallow, and it actually hurt. She took a huge breath and turned to face him full on. "*Dat*, there's something I have to tell you."

"Well, out with it, then. I'm hungry."

She should wait until he was fed. He might take it better, but she was too nervous to wait.

"I'm leaving," she blurted.

"Huh? You just got home. Where are you going? Make me a hot supper first, at the very least."

"I'll make you a hot supper. And I'm not leaving tonight. I'm leaving tomorrow."

"Two days in a row? I don't think so, daughter." He sat down on a kitchen bench and gazed at her.

"Not just for tomorrow," she said, hating the quiver in her voice.

His eyes had widened now, and his forehead was creasing. "What do you mean?"

"I have taken a job in Hollybrook—"

He jumped up from the table. "What? What's this?"

She immediately shrank back from him, and then with trembling determination, she squared her shoulders. "I've taken a job caring for two young *kinner* and helping around the house."

He was gawking at her. His cheeks had turned red. "What? I don't understand."

"I've taken a job caring for two—"

"I heard you," he snapped. "What job? With who? How did you find out about it?"

She couldn't tell him that his favorite niece had told her about it. She couldn't do that to Greta. "I just heard about it, and I went to Hollybrook today and got the job. I leave tomorrow."

For a wretched moment, he said nothing, just stared at her. "You were to be with Greta."

"There was a change of plans."

"But Abner brought you—"

"He gave me a ride home from the bus station."

"Did Greta—"

"I went alone." Her stomach hurt. Despite wanting to leave home with every fiber of her being, she felt a huge, unexpected wave of sympathy for her father. But he dispelled that instantly when he went on.

"And what of me? What of *your job* here?"

She stared at him. Her *job*? "My job here?" she cried. "So that is all it's been. Everything I've done? A job? Well, you can hire someone else to do it. And I suggest you pay them this time."

As the words poured from her mouth, she nearly buckled. How could she be so brazen with her father? How could she speak to him in such a tone?

"Get out," he said. "Get *out*. You can leave tonight if you're in such a hurry."

He gave her a scathing look and turned on his heel and stomped from the room. He clumped through the washroom and out of the house. She stood there, breathing hard. Tears filled her eyes and slowly trickled down her cheeks.

It was done. Her father knew she was leaving.

Where was the ecstasy she had thought she'd feel? Where was the elation? For right then, all she felt was sick to her stomach.

She turned slowly around and mechanically began to fix his dinner. She'd leave it on the stove warm and then she'd gather her things and leave. She had nowhere to go but Greta's. Her aunt and uncle would open their home to her. She'd spent many a night there in the past. She could pretend it was a sleep-over.

Yes. That was all it was. A sleep-over.

∼

"Lucy? You awake?"

Lucy stirred in the bed and opened her eyes. Greta was leaning over her.

"It's getting late. I know you didn't sleep much last night, but still... *Mamm* and *Dat* will wonder if you don't come down and help prepare breakfast."

"Right," Lucy muttered, sitting up. "*Jah.* Thanks. I'll be down in a minute."

"Okay. I'll tell *Mamm*." Greta gave her a sympathetic smile and left the bedroom.

Lucy felt stiff all over. It was true; she hadn't slept much more than an hour or two all night. She couldn't get that last look of her father out of her mind. It was not only full of loathing, but there was something else, and it had looked an awful lot like hurt. That was what troubled her.

Behind all his harshness, had her father been hurt she was leaving—that she wanted to leave? It seemed unlikely. But she couldn't shake the idea. She'd expected the anger and maybe even some hatred. But she hadn't expected him to be hurt—it had never even crossed her mind.

She swung her legs off the mattress and stood up. She couldn't and wouldn't fret about it now; it was done. There was no going back, and she needed to get on with the day. She was expected in Hollybrook. Today, her entire life was changing. She resolutely pushed thoughts of her father out of her mind and smiled. It was going to be a good change. Hadn't God directed her in it?

She hurried down the hallway to the bathroom to get ready. She was taking the morning bus. Josh was going to pay her back the fare. He seemed nice. Certainly, nicer than her father. But there was Tamar. No matter. Lucy shook her head. One thing at a time. And right now, she had to get ready, go downstairs, and help with breakfast. That was enough for this hour.

## Chapter Nine

Josh glanced at the clock above the cooking stove. He needed to get going shortly or he wouldn't be there to meet Lucy's bus. And he didn't want her to have to start walking. That would be no way for her to start her job with his family. He had high hopes. Already, Cornelia loved her, and Cornelia could be somewhat stubborn with new people. But she'd taken to Lucy straight away. And David—well, David would go along with the prevailing opinion. The thought was somewhat troubling. Ever since his mother had died, David didn't have his own opinion on much. Oh, he'd argue gladly with Cornelia, but in other ways, he didn't make much of a stand in what he thought. And Josh wanted him to be a strong boy, to know what was right and wrong, to stand up for what was right. To stand up for what he believed.

He shook his head impatiently. Goodness, the boy was only four years old. He didn't need strong opinions yet. But still, the thought bothered him.

*Sara,* he thought, *what do you think of Greta? Do you like her? Did I do right to hire her?*

"What are you standing there for? You look like a fence post," his mother told him.

"*Ach*, you're right. I'm gathering wool." He smiled at her and handed her the basket of eggs, which was why he was in the kitchen in the first place.

"Gather wool out in the field," Tamar said. "There's lots to be done out there."

"You're right at that," he agreed pleasantly. "I do need to fetch Lucy, though. She's coming on the early bus, and she's almost here."

Tamar sniffed and turned to the sink.

"You'll give her a chance, won't you?" he asked.

"I said I would."

"I know what you said, but truly... You will give her a chance?"

Tamar turned to face him. "I said I would. I still think it's a huge waste of money, and I'm thinking *Gott* don't like it when we waste our resources."

Josh sighed. "Maybe so. But we're going to give this a fair try, nevertheless."

Cornelia came running into the kitchen. "I wanna know how to read," she said, placing her little fists on her waist.

"Read?" Josh asked, biting back his smile at her defiant pose. "What's brought that on?"

"I wanna read to Lucy when she comes. I don't want her thinkin' I'm a *boppli*."

"I ain't a *boppli*, neither," said David, who had followed Cornelia into the kitchen.

"You're both growing up right fast," Josh said. "And come next fall, you'll be starting school, Cornelia, so you'll be reading soon enough."

"But I wanna read now." She looked at her grandmother. "*Mammi*, will you teach me? You know how."

Tamar clucked her tongue. "You think I've got time to be teaching you to read? That's what we got the school for. You just need to be patient. It'll come soon enough."

Cornelia scowled. "But—"

"That's enough, Cornelia. You can tell Lucy stories instead. Now, who wants to go with me to pick her up from the bus?"

"I do," Cornelia cried with excitement.

David echoed her sentiment. "Me, too."

"Then go on out to the barn. We'll hitch up the buggy and be on our way." He looked at his mother. "Do you want to come? There's room."

"I know there's room. It's your *dat's* buggy, after all. And *nee*. I won't be going. I have plenty to keep me busy."

"It'd be nice if you did come, *Mamm*. A real nice welcome for her."

"You three are welcome enough," Tamar said, placing the fresh eggs into a glass bowl. "I'll see her soon enough."

Josh went to his mother and put his arm around her shoulders and squeezed her in a gentle hug. "Thanks, *Mamm*."

His mother looked at him with tears in her eyes. "Go on with you," she said, her voice breaking only a little. "You'll be late."

He smiled at her and left the house.

∽

Lucy wanted to chew her fingernails when the bus pulled into the town of Hollybrook, but she didn't. She'd finally weened herself from that habit when she was twenty-three years old, and she wasn't of a mind to start it up again. Still, she was nervous, and she wanted something to do with her hands. She folded them and pressed them hard into her lap. This was it. She'd waited for this day for a long time, and now it was here.

83

She wondered briefly what her father was doing. She'd hoped to speak with him about bringing someone in to help with the cooking and cleaning. In truth, she'd already thought of a few suggestions—all lovely, kind women who lived alone. Their names had come to her on the bus ride home. She thought any of them would be thrilled to have a part-time position and the opportunity to make a bit of extra cash.

But the way it turned out, she didn't have a chance to talk to him about anything. She didn't even have a chance to say a proper good-bye. Well, she could write him, couldn't she? If he wouldn't talk to her, he might still read her letters. Especially since he could do so without her even knowing.

She had left quite a good supply of groceries in the house, as she'd gone to the market earlier that week. She was happy about that. He wouldn't starve, at least. She had a hard time imaging her father going to the market and buying groceries for himself. He'd consider that women's work—all the more reason to get someone in to help.

She would write him a letter that very evening, giving him her suggestions. He likely wouldn't take them well, but he was a practical man underneath all his bluster. He'd see the wisdom in it, and hopefully, he'd get right on it. She was particularly fond of the idea of Martha Brenner helping him. The woman was down to earth, hard-working, and patient. Her dad would need all her qualities. And Martha was strong emotionally—and she would need to be if she was to work for Bartholomew Oyer.

Lucy glanced out the window just as the bus came grinding to a halt. There was a scattering of buggies about—others likely waiting for passengers. Was one of them Josh? She hoped so. But then, she could always start walking.

She got off the bus and waited while the driver unlatched the storage area beneath the bus. He fished her suitcase out for her.

"I'll carry that for you," Josh said to her.

She turned quickly and gave him a reserved smile—not too warm, as she'd decided that things between this widower and her must be kept formal at all times. Not that she assumed they wouldn't; but she wasn't about to take any chances. She had no interest whatsoever in things ever becoming confused or in any possibility of budding feelings between them.

The children were jumping up and down on the backseat of the buggy waiting for her.

"You're here," Cornelia cried. "*Dat* said we had to wait inside."

"I'm so glad to see you, Nellie," Lucy said. "And you, too, David. How are you?"

"We're right *gut*," Cornelia said with a grin. "I was going to learn to read before you got here, but I couldn't."

"Oh, were you?" Lucy said. She heard Josh chuckle, and she looked over at him. There was a twinkle in his eye as he gazed back at his daughter.

"I don't know how to read, neither," David lamented.

"Well, I can read. So if there is anything to be read, I will read it to you." Lucy set her purse down at the floor by her feet.

"You're gonna live with us now," Cornelia said. "But you ain't our *mamm*."

Lucy's heart caught. "*Nee*," she said tenderly. "I ain't your *mamm*."

"We don't got a *mamm* anymore," David said. "She's in heaven."

"But she will always be your *mamm*. And I imagine she's right proud of you," Lucy ventured softly.

"Pride's a sin," Cornelia announced.

"*Ach*, Cornelia, Lucy wasn't talking about that kind of pride," Josh said.

He looked distinctly uncomfortable, and Lucy quickly thought of something else to say. "I could teach you a bit of reading."

Cornelia leaned so forward on her seat, she nearly fell off. "You could? *Dat*? Did you hear that?"

"I heard." He turned to Lucy. "You don't need to fret about it. She'll be in school come fall."

Did he not want her to teach Cornelia? Or did he think she wasn't capable? Or—

"The girl comes up with new ideas every minute," he said, interrupting her thoughts. "I don't want you thinking you have to do them all."

Lucy smiled. "All right. I'm sure we'll be fine."

"But *Dat*, I wanna read."

He rolled his eyes in exasperation. "Cornelia, why don't you look out the window and count the buggies you see."

Lucy laughed. "My *mamm* used to have me do the same."

His brow rose. "Did she now?"

Shortly, they were turning into the drive at the house.

"We're home," Cornelia said. "I wonder if *Mammi* made cookies."

Lucy couldn't help but laugh. The girl was going to keep her on her toes, for sure and for certain.

"I wanna cookie," David said.

"There will be no cookies now," Josh told them. "It's nearly time for the noon meal."

Lucy bit the corner of her lip. She was here. Her new home. She sent up a quick prayer, not only of thanksgiving but of supplication. She wanted to be a blessing to these children. And she wanted to get along well with their grandmother. As for the father? She glanced at him.

Well, she wanted to get along with him, too, but mostly, she just wanted to keep her distance. She had a funny feeling when she looked at him. One she couldn't exactly explain. Was she feeling pity for him—being widowed so young and having the *kinner* alone? Was it caution—and if so, why? He had been nothing but kind and, well, normal, with her. Why should that make her uneasy? He wasn't her father.

But she felt edgy just the same.

Folks in her district of Marksville didn't really know what her father was like. Even Greta and her family didn't really know what her father was like. So, it was entirely possible that Josh wasn't as he appeared to be.

Best err on the side of caution.

The children tore straight into the house after Josh pulled the buggy to a stop by the barn. She got out a bit more slowly.

"Go on to the house," Josh told her. "I'll unhitch Crafty and bring up your luggage when I come."

"I can take it."

"I know you can. But let me." He began unbuckling the leather straps.

She let out her breath and then turned toward the house. Squaring her shoulders, she went to the front porch and then climbed the steps, letting herself inside. She knew the family used the side door and that the front was left for visitors. But she felt like a visitor. With time, she'd go in and out of the side door with the rest of them.

She heard the children chattering with Tamar in the kitchen. She hung her purse on a peg by the door and followed their voices.

"Hello," she said, entering the kitchen and putting on a bright smile for Tamar.

Tamar's gray eyes met hers. "Hello."

At least she'd greeted her, Lucy thought. "I'd like to help with the noon meal. What do you need me to do?"

"I don't need you to do anything," Tamar snapped and then she stopped and took a slow breath. "You could fill the glasses with milk and set them on the table."

"Of course," Lucy said.

"I can help," Cornelia said, rushing to the counter and grabbing two glasses.

"Don't you be dropping those," Tamar admonished her.

"I won't."

"I can help, too," David said.

"*Ach*, this ain't no place for lads," Tamar said. "Go on out and help your *dat*."

This suited David fine, and he scampered off to join his father. Lucy and Cornelia filled the glasses with milk and set them on the table in the dining area.

"What else can I do?" Lucy asked. With time, she wouldn't ask what needed to be done. She'd just take care of things. But now, after only just arriving, she wanted to be careful not to step on Tamar's toes. It was her kitchen, after all, and she didn't seem too pleased to have it invaded.

Tamar stood as if she were considering what Lucy could do. "Why don't you get settled in? Cornelia can show you your room."

Lucy had been dismissed. She kept a smile on her face and nodded. "*Gut* idea," she said.

Cornelia had grabbed her hand and was dragging her out of the kitchen. "Your bedroom is right next to mine. I could sleep with you, though, if you get lonely."

Lucy laughed. "Thank you, but I'll be fine. I need to get my luggage."

Just then, Josh came through, carrying her suitcase. "I'll take this on up."

He started up the stairs, and Cornelia and Lucy followed him. He walked into the second bedroom on the left and put the suitcase on the double bed covered with a yellow and blue quilt.

"This is your room. Do you like it?" Cornelia asked. "Wanna see my room?"

"Goodness, Cornelia. Let the woman get settled in first." He gazed at Lucy. "Will it suit?"

Lucy glanced around the sparse room. It was clean, almost painfully clean. She looked forward to putting her hand mirror and her journal on the dresser to make it feel a bit more homey.

"It suits fine, thank you."

"*Gut*. Then I'll leave you to it," he said, nodding and leaving the room.

Cornelia grabbed her hand. "Wanna see my room now?"

"How about you help me unpack first."

Cornelia's eyes lit up. "*Jah!* I'll help."

Together, they hung her dresses on the pegs running along the wall. Then they filled the first two drawers of the dresser.

"That all you got?" Cornelia asked.

"It's plenty," Lucy assured her, smiling. A person didn't need much in the way of clothing. Plus, she had two aprons which helped her dresses last longer between washings.

"Okay, now my room."

Cornelia led the way next door to her room. It looked pretty much the same as Lucy's except there was a doll on the bed.

"Do you like dolls?" Cornelia asked.

"I love dolls. I've made a few."

Cornelia's eyes grew large. "You have? For who? You got *kinner?*"

"*Nee.* I don't have any *kinner.* I'm not married, Nellie. I've made them for the *kinner* of my friends."

"Can I make one?"

"We'll see." Lucy put her hand on Cornelia's shoulder. "It'd be fun, but I need to see how my days go first. I want to be a big help to your *mammi.*"

Cornelia frowned. "Sometimes, *Mammi* gets mad."

Lucy hesitated, then said, "I think she's sad because your *daadi* passed on."

"But my *mamm* did, too. And I'm not mad." Her voice broke. "I'm just sad."

She leaned against Lucy, and Lucy put her arms around her. "I know you are. And it's all right to be sad."

"But I want to cry sometimes." She pulled away and looked tearfully into Lucy's eyes. "I cry at night sometimes, but I don't want *Dat* to hear me."

"Why not?"

"Cause then he'll be sad all over again."

"It's all right if he knows you're crying."

Cornelia shook her head. "*Nee*, it ain't. And don't you tell him I cry. You won't, will you?" She became anxious.

"I won't tell a soul."

Cornelia threw her arms around Lucy. "I knew you were nice. I knew it."

Lucy laughed and gave her a long squeeze. "Shall we go back downstairs? I want to see if your *mammi* needs help putting the meal on the table."

"I don't think she wants your help," Cornelia said straightforwardly as she walked out of the room.

# Chapter Ten

Bartholomew Oyer opened his eyes to darkness. The sun hadn't come up quite yet. Still, there was no reason to be dawdling. But he didn't move; his limbs felt leaden. What in the world was the matter with him?

And then, he remembered. Lucy was gone. His daughter had up and left him. Like he was no better than a worn-out shoe. She'd simply taken a job and left. He hadn't even known she was looking for a job. And why would she, anyway? She had a home here with him. He fed her, didn't he? He gave her a bed and a roof. Why in the world would she have any desire to leave?

The ungrateful child.

And that look on her face when she'd told him. A mixture of glee and fear. She'd been happy to go. As if he meant nothing.

How in the world was he supposed to run the house and the farm without her? Impossible. That was what it was. Downright impossible.

And Lucy had to know that. She had to know he wouldn't be able to do it. But she didn't care. She just up and left.

He clenched his jaw and made himself get up. The wooden floor was cool on his feet, despite it being a warm spring. He tromped over to his dresser and took out a clean shirt. And who was going to do the laundry now? He didn't know how to work that wringer washer. He'd never touched it in his life. A lone dress hanging on a peg behind the door caught his eye.

"She's gone, Janet," he muttered to his deceased wife. "Gone. Just like you."

But it wasn't just like her, was it? Janet was dead, and he would never see her again. Lucy was very much alive. He could go straight to Hollybrook and fetch her home. He was the head of the household, placed there by God himself. Whatever family she was working for would know that and release her immediately.

*She's twenty-seven years old,* he thought. *Old enough to be on her own.*

Why hadn't she married, anyway? He supposed she was normal looking, maybe even pretty if she ever smiled. He had always figured she and her husband could live with him; then he'd have a helper out in the fields. It would have worked out right fine.

What was the girl thinking?

He thought again about the fear in her eyes. Why was she afraid? Because she knew she was wrong to leave. That had to be it. But he'd seen that look in her eyes before—when she hadn't had a thing to announce to him. Was Lucy afraid of him? He was her *dat*. And sometimes, he had to be hard on her. He had to teach her. It was his full responsibility. She didn't have a *mamm* anymore.

He changed into his fresh shirt and pulled on his somewhat dirty trousers. He snatched up his suspenders and clipped them in place. Lord, he was hungry. And then it hit him again. Lucy wasn't here. There would be no hot breakfast waiting for him when he came in from the barn. What was he supposed to eat, anyway? Surely, he didn't have to fix his own eggs.

But he did.

And he would have to from now on. He swallowed the bitterness in his mouth. *This is your fault, Janet. If you hadn't up and died, I wouldn't be in this mess.*

He tromped down the hallway to the bathroom. This was going to be a rotten day.

∽

Lucy jumped out of bed and hurriedly changed. She wanted to be the first one downstairs, so she needed to get a move on. The day before had gone well enough. She even felt that Tamar was making somewhat of an effort, which Lucy dearly appreciated. Lucy wanted to give her no reason to find fault. She'd tread carefully in the kitchen, making sure she didn't step on Tamar's feet. But with the children, she could take more control. She'd work to keep them busy and entertained.

*Ach,* but Cornelia was something. Lucy already adored her, even as she realized the girl's strong and stubborn spirit. But there was tenderness there, too. A sweetness that made Cornelia even more precious.

"You up?" Cornelia asked, sticking her head into the room.

Lucy laughed. "I see you are."

"David's still sleeping. I checked."

"Did you now?"

"You ain't dressed."

"I will be if you'll give me a minute."

Cornelia giggled. "Okay," she said and withdrew from the room.

Lucy got dressed quickly, glad she'd used the bathroom earlier, and when she left her room, she saw Cornelia waiting for her in the hallway with her back pressed against the wall. The little girl smiled. "You're ready now."

"I'm ready now. Let's go downstairs and see if we can give your *mammi* a hand."

Cornelia began skipping down the hallway. "All right. I like to cook."

"I'm sure you do," Lucy said, laughing and walking faster to keep up with the child.

In the kitchen, Tamar was pulling out the iron skillet from beneath the stove. She looked up when they entered, grunting a hello. Cornelia ran to her and gave her a hug.

"We're gonna help you cook breakfast."

Tamar's mouth tightened slightly. "And what if I don't need no help?"

Cornelia laughed with glee. "Everybody wants help," she said sagely. "And I can scramble the eggs right *gut*. 'Member, I did it the other day."

Tamar's expression softened and she chuckled. "*Jah*, I remember."

"Shall I slice the bread and start some toast?" Lucy asked, hanging back.

Tamar didn't look at her. "Suit yourself."

"That means you can do it," Cornelia interpreted.

Goodness, but the child had a comment for everything. Lucy went to the counter and took a loaf of bread from the breadbox. She found a serrated knife and began cutting thin, even slices. Then she found a cookie sheet and arranged the bread on it. In the meantime, Cornelia had pulled a chair to the stove and was standing on it, stirring the scrambled eggs with a wooden spatula as they began to cook in the skillet.

Tamar moved about with the ease of a woman who had spent her entire life in the kitchen. Lucy carefully maneuvered around her. She found the utensils and the dishes and set the table for the five of them.

Cornelia kept up a continual stream of chatter, whether anyone responded to her or not. David came shuffling into the kitchen a few minutes later.

"*Gut* morning, David," Lucy said cheerfully.

"You ain't got dressed," Tamar said, clucking her tongue. "Go on up and get your clothes on."

David looked at her as if he were still half asleep.

"C'mon, David," Lucy said, extending her hand. When he grabbed it, she continued, "I'll go back up with you."

She thought she heard Tamar sniff when they left the kitchen, but she couldn't be sure. No matter. The children were her responsibility, and besides, she wanted to spend a few minutes with David alone. They hadn't had much chance yet to form a relationship.

"It's going to be a *gut* day," she told the sleepy boy as they went into his room. "Hmmm. I see your bed ain't made. Shall we do it together?"

David's brow crinkled. "I don't make the bed."

Lucy laughed. "Let's do it together. Here, you pull up the quilt like this..."

Within seconds, the bed was made. Lucy helped David choose a shirt. She helped him get dressed and then combed his hair.

"You look right handsome," she said with a smile.

He scowled.

"What's wrong?"

"You think *Mamm* can see me?" he asked.

Lucy swallowed. "I think your *mamm* is watching over you," she said softly. "She still loves you even though she ain't here anymore."

"I don't see why *Gott* gets her in heaven. I want her here."

Lucy knelt beside him and put her hands on his shoulders. "I know you do, David. And I'm sure she misses you, too."

His brow rose. "You think so? You think she misses me? She didn't forget me?"

"*Ach, nee.* She could never forget you. Never in a million years."

His eyes welled up with tears. He sniffed and wiped at them. "Let's go back downstairs," he said.

She stood. "*Jah.* Let's go see how breakfast is coming along."

He put his hand in hers, and her breath caught. What a dear, sweet, little boy. She was already falling in love with him. How blessed she was to be here, to be part of his life.

For a moment, her thoughts went to her father. How she wished she had tender feelings for him. As she went down the steps, she searched her heart. She knew somewhere deep inside, she loved him. He was her father. Years ago, they had gotten along fine—when she was little, and her mother was still alive. But it had been such a long, long time ago, she could hardly remember it. Those days were as if they belonged to another life. Another person.

A different father.

A wave of sadness swept over her for what had been lost. She had tried. She had tried and tried and tried. She consoled herself with that, but the feeling of having failed remained.

David tugged on her hand, and she looked down into his wide brown eyes. "We got a tire swing. You wanna push me in it later?"

"I want to very much," she told him, shoving aside the thoughts of her father.

"It's all ready," Cornelia announced when she spotted Lucy and David.

"It smells right *gut*," Lucy commented.

"Wanna go tell *Dat?*" Cornelia asked her. "I gotta get out the honey and put it on the table."

"Surely, your *dat* will be in soon."

"*Mammi* said the eggs will get cold."

Lucy sighed. "All right. David, you want to go out with me?"

"*Mammi* wants him to wash up."

Mammi seemed to have a lot to say that morning about things. Lucy put on a smile. What was the matter with her? It was no big task to call Josh in for breakfast. Chances were, she'd have to do it many times over the next months.

"I'll be right back," she said, and slipped out the front door. She walked straight to the barn and entering, she paused for a moment to adjust to the shadowy interior. She spotted Josh balancing a huge sack of feed on one shoulder. He must have stepped on something, for he faltered and looked about to go down.

Lucy ran across the barn and caught one end of the bag before it hit the floor. Together, they balanced it.

"*Ach,* thanks for that," Josh said, shaking his head. "I almost dropped it, and I reckon it would have burst open."

She laughed. "That would not have been fun to clean up."

"You're right at that." He hefted the bag more firmly into his grip. "You can let go if you want."

"Where are you heading with it?"

"Just over there." He gestured with his head to the corner of the barn.

"I can help," she said, and together they stepped over to the corner.

"Okay, let's lower it," Josh said.

They lowered it carefully onto a stack of other grain bags. Lucy was painfully aware of how close Josh was to her. She could even feel his breath flutter over her face, and she could breathe in his aroma of barn and outdoors and work.

When he eased his hands from under the bag, he accidentally brushed against her arm. His touch sent a jolt through her, and she jumped back. He noticed and even in the morning shadow, she could see his face go red. She felt like a fool. It was a mere touch, no more, and she'd reacted as if he'd slapped her or something. Now she could feel her own face go red.

"Sorry," he muttered.

She took another step back. "Breakfast is ready. Your *mamm* doesn't want it to get cold." And with that, she turned and hurried out of the barn and back across the yard and into the house. If she was going to live with this family, she was going to have to learn how to act around the father. She rolled her eyes with disgust.

"Get yourself in hand," she whispered just inside the door.

Josh came in through the washroom and during breakfast, Lucy made sure they didn't have eye contact. She focused solely on the children, which suited them and her. But at the end of the meal, Josh spoke to her.

"Lucy, do you have everything you need?"

She blinked. "*Jah.* Of course. Everything's fine."

"You'll let me know if there's anything?"

"She said she's fine," Tamar interjected.

"I hear her, *Mamm.* I was just checking."

"I *am* fine," Lucy said, forcing a smile. "No cause to fret."

She jumped up and began clearing the table. As she took a stack of dishes into the kitchen, she heard David chatting with Josh about helping in the fields.

Cornelia came in, carrying empty glasses. "I gotta help with the dishes," she said. "*Mammi* told me."

"I'll help, too. It won't take any time at all." Lucy peered through the kitchen window. "Does your *mammi* have a garden? I haven't explored behind the house yet."

Cornelia shrugged. "I don't know."

"I do have a garden," Tamar said.

"Have you planted it yet? I know it's still fairly early."

"Some things are planted. We could still have a frost."

"*Jah,* that is so. I love to garden. I hope you'll let me help."

Tamar shrugged, but she didn't say no. Lucy took it as a victory. Smiling now, she glanced down at Cornelia.

"After the dishes, let's take a few minutes to swing. I promised David I'd push him."

Cornelia grinned. "And then you can teach me to read."

Tamar snorted, and Lucy laughed. "It only it were that easy," Lucy said. "But we can practice the alphabet together. Do you know it?"

Cornelia frowned mightily. "I don't even know what it is."

"All right. We'll start there. I can teach you a song."

Cornelia's face cleared, and Lucy grabbed a dish towel to start drying the dishes Cornelia was beginning to wash. Tamar stood for a moment, watching them. Lucy wanted to tell her to go rest, but she feared such a comment wouldn't be appreciated, so she kept quiet.

Tamar remained for a few more seconds, and then she left the room.

"Can I have a cookie?" Cornelia asked. "I been doing a lot of work around here."

"You think you've earned one?"

Cornelia nodded vigorously. "*Jah.* I earned one."

"Maybe a little bit later. We just finished our meal, after all. Besides, it's awfully early in the day."

"I don't think so," Cornelia said, setting down a dry plate. "It ain't never too early for a cookie."

Lucy shook her head in amusement. "I'm right certain you wouldn't think it's ever too early."

## Chapter Eleven

Josh left the barn to head out to the fields. He needed to check a fence line. In truth, he had half a notion to pull the fence out. He seemed to remember this fence had been in place years before when his father had bought the land. He certainly had no recollection of his father putting a fence up. Most folks had no fences at all, which was the way he preferred it. Less to keep up and manage, for sure and for certain.

As he passed the house, he glanced toward the kitchen window. He could see movement inside, but he couldn't really make out who it was. His *mamm*, surely, and likely Lucy and Cornelia. *Ach*, that had been awkward when his arm had brushed against Lucy earlier. She hadn't liked it either. It was as if his touch had insulted her somehow, which was odd. It wasn't like he'd done it on purpose. He would never have touched her on purpose, for they hardly knew each other, and it wouldn't have been appropriate.

Something must have happened for her to be so jumpy.

Or maybe, it was just that she was new here. Either way, he'd be extra careful not to let it happen again. He couldn't have her running off just as the *kinner* were getting used to her. And besides, he didn't want her to leave. There was a toughness in Lucy, a strength that would surely win over his mother before too long. Or so he hoped.

And if Lucy couldn't win her over, he shuddered to think of having to try all over again with someone else.

Goodness, but he hoped he hadn't offended her.

If only Sara was here. She'd know what Lucy was feeling—she had a keen sense of intuition about such things. But then, if Sara was here, there would be no need for Lucy at all. Again, that familiar empty feeling of being alone swooped through him. He sighed, tired of how the sensation was never far from his awareness. Mentally, he shoved it away and focused on the task at hand.

⁓

Bartholomew Oyer vacillated between anger and loneliness. He hadn't realized just how much he'd depended on Lucy for basic companionship. Not that they ever really talked—except about what needed to be done. But she'd been there—

a steady presence in the home. And she worked hard keeping things up. He knew it was a hard task all by herself, but that was just the way things were.

He supposed he could have told her now and again that she did a good job, but he couldn't let her be vain, now, could he? He was her father. If she turned vain, it would come back on him. Besides, he worked hard, too. Life was hard work, and the sooner Lucy realized it, the better off she'd be. It was his job to make sure of that.

And he had made sure of it, hadn't he? He kept her busy from sun-up to sun-down. He wondered if she was working as hard at her so-called job. He gritted his teeth and his hands tightened into fists.

How dare she leave him like this. High and dry, she'd left him. Like he had never done a thing for her. Like he hadn't sheltered her or fed her. Like he hadn't taken care of everything in her life. Like he hadn't...

He ran out of steam, then, and slouched against the wooden slats of the rocking chair. He was hungry. He'd made himself a peanut butter and jelly sandwich for supper, but he longed for a real meal. A hot meal—one that would stick to his ribs.

Lucy was a fine cook. She'd even surpassed her mother in that, truth be told. Was she cooking for this other family now?

Instantly, his anger returned. She should be here, cooking for him.

The cursed girl. Running off like that. He should go fetch her back. *Jah,* that was what he should do. Fetch her back where she belonged. He was certain all the menfolk would agree with him on that. He was the head of the household; Lucy had no right to run off like she had.

He bolted out of the chair and began pacing the room. He could go the next day and bring her home. He wasn't sure exactly where she was, for there hadn't been time to receive any letters.

But then, would she write? She should write immediately to tell him how she was and exactly where she was. But no. There probably wouldn't be one word from her. *Ach,* but the girl was insufferable. If her mother could see her now, she'd be ashamed.

He stopped pacing and swallowed. Would she? Would his Janet really be ashamed of Lucy? Or would she be ashamed of *him*? Would she see it differently? Would she tell him he'd chased Lucy away?

No. No. That couldn't be right.

He started pacing again, clenching his hands behind his back. He'd go get her. He'd go get Lucy. Maybe not the next day, but surely within a week or so. Surely.

# THE RECENT WIDOWER

Lucy's days settled into a sort of routine. Tamar seemed all right with her taking over the care of the children. Oh, she'd fuss with them now and again and even read them a story or two at times, but other than that, tending them fell to Lucy.

Lucy was able to help with the meals—not greatly, but enough to feel as if she were contributing something. She'd also taken to keeping the floors swept, but she didn't dare touch the dust rag. She'd learned her lesson on that one.

"Don't touch that," Tamar had cried when Lucy had picked up a carved boy to dust under it.

Lucy had nearly dropped the wooden carving in surprise. "I-I... Well, it's dusty, and I thought I could get at it better by moving it."

"Don't touch it," Tamar had repeated, bustling across the room to snatch it from her hands. And then she had snatched the dust rag from her, too. "You leave the dusting to me. Go on, now. Do something else."

Lucy had backed away, feeling like a scolded child. Cornelia, who had been watching, stared with wide eyes.

"*Mammi*," she started, "how come—"

But Lucy had grabbed her hand and pulled her from the room.

"*Mammi* is all mad," Cornelia said. "And all you was doing was helping."

"It's fine," Lucy said, injecting a light tone into her voice. "Your *mammi* likes to dust, so that's just fine with me."

Cornelia giggled then. "Now, you got less work to do. Can we go outside and play?"

"That we can," Lucy said, relieved to be getting out of the house. "Let's go get David. He's with your *dat* in the barn."

So they went to the barn. Josh and David were forking straw into the stalls. At least, Josh was. David appeared to be just getting in the way.

"David," called Lucy. "Would you like to swing or play tag?"

David grinned and hurried over to them.

"Can I speak with you for a moment?" Josh asked.

Lucy tensed. Had she done something wrong? What could he want? Her mind whirled over her actions over the last day or two, but she could think of nothing.

"Go on out to the yard," Josh told his children. "Lucy will be right there."

Lucy stood stiffly as the children left the barn. Josh moved close but seemed careful to maintain a good distance between them.

"Have I done something wrong?" she asked. Visions of her father's disgruntled face filled her mind.

"What?" Josh asked, looking perplexed. "*Nee*? Why would you think so?"

"Because…" She suddenly felt foolish. "Well, you wanted to talk to me."

"I do want to talk to you, but only to ask how things are going. As I told you in the beginning, *Mamm* can be difficult sometimes." His eyes were earnest on hers. He really did care how things were going for her. The realization was somewhat startling to Lucy.

"They're … everything is going fine."

"So, *Mamm* and you are getting along?" He looked so hopeful, she couldn't help but smile.

"I don't know about that. But she is abiding me. Except…" She hesitated, wondering if she should ask about the carved boy.

"Except what?" he asked, now concerned. "Has something happened?"

She shook her head. "Not really. I was just wondering about the carved boy in the front room."

"Ahh," he said slowly, and a look of understanding crossed his face. "That boy is me."

"What?"

He smiled, clearly enjoying his memory. "*Dat* carved it of me when I was ten years old. It was his favorite carving. He always wanted it in the front room where he could see it come evening time. Most of his carvings we could play with, but not that one. He was right possessive of it."

"Oh," she said softly. Now, it was making more sense.

"I s'pose it means a lot to *Mamm* now, what with *Dat* gone." He was quiet for a moment before speaking again. "I appreciate how well you're doing with the *kinner*. They like you. You've helped them … helped them adjust. I'm grateful."

She could feel her cheeks go hot with his compliment. She hadn't expected it, but she was gratified to hear it. "I-I," she stammered. Then she cleared her throat. "It's easy. Your *kinner* are wonderful."

He laughed out loud at that. "*Gut* to hear. Even my Cornelia, or Nellie as she demands I call her?"

Lucy laughed. "I'm sorry about that. I didn't mean for that nickname to cause problems."

"*Ach*, it doesn't. It just amuses me. I think her mother would have liked it."

Lucy's brow rose. It wasn't often she heard Josh say anything about his late wife. "I hope so."

"Cornelia seems more settled. You wouldn't notice, not having seen her before. But you're *gut* for her."

Lucy nodded, embarrassed now. "Is that... Is that all?"

He looked momentarily surprised, as if she were dismissing him. Her face was flaming hot now. Goodness, but she was talking too much. He would think her impertinent.

"*Jah.* That's all. I'm glad you're settling in. Let me know if you need anything."

"All right," she said and hurried out of the barn. She touched her cheek, feeling the heat there. What a strange interaction. She'd thought she was in trouble and he was going to reproach her for something. Instead, he'd complimented her—she hardly knew how to respond.

But at least, her job seemed secure at the moment. In truth, she liked it here and hoped to stay for a long time. Until Josh remarried, for she was certain he would. He was handsome and kind, and his children were adorable. It wouldn't be long before the single women took notice.

And then, Lucy's days here would be numbered. She sighed. Well, it hadn't happened yet, so she was going to enjoy every day until it did.

# Chapter Twelve

❦

The day had gone calmly. The children were involved in weeding a corner of the garden. Lucy was watching over them to assure they didn't disturb any vegetables. She'd gotten permission from Tamar to be out there in the garden in the first place, and she certainly didn't want to do anything to jeopardize future involvement.

"Is this a weed?" Cornelia asked, pointing to a carrot pushing through the dirt.

"*Ach! Nee*, that's a carrot. Don't touch that."

Just then, a piercing scream came from inside the house. Lucy gasped and went running. It had to be Tamar. No one else was in the house. She threw open the side screen door and raced inside.

"Tamar!" she cried. "Where are you?"

She heard whimpering from the front room and nearly slipped in her hurry to get there. Tamar was lying on the floor, her face blanched, and her eyes screwed up in pain.

"*Ach!* Tamar!" Lucy flew to her and knelt beside her. "Where does it hurt?"

Tamar's eyes were frantic as she looked up at Lucy. "My-my hip."

Lucy sucked in a breath. "All right. I'll get help." She pulled an afghan off the davenport and tucked it around Tamar. "I'll get help. I'll hurry."

"*Mammi!*" both Cornelia and David cried as they rushed into the room. "Did you fall down?" Cornelia asked.

"You stay with her. Don't touch her," Lucy directed. She hurried from the house, running to the field. She spotted Josh in the northeast corner. She ran to him, hollering, "Josh! Josh!"

He heard her almost immediately and came running to meet her.

"What? What is it?" he asked, his face white.

Lucy gasped in air. "Your *mamm*. She's fallen. She's hurt her hip."

He took off toward the house, and she followed at his heels. He burst through the side door and followed the voices of his children to the front room.

"*Mamm*."

Tamar gazed over at him, looking incredibly frail and helpless. Her mouth was pinched.

"I-I fell."

"I see that. I'll call for an ambulance." He looked at Lucy. "Stay with her. The phone shanty ain't far."

And he was gone.

Lucy hurried to Tamar and knelt beside her once again. "Do you want some water?"

Tamar shook her head, clearly unable to muster the strength to talk any further.

"Is she okay?" Cornelia asked, tugging on Lucy's sleeve.

"She's going to be fine," Lucy said. "Your *dat* is getting help. The doctors will fix her right up."

"But *Mamm* died," David said, his eyes huge with fear. He stuck his fingers in his mouth and began sucking on them frantically.

"*Jah*, she did. And I know you are still sad about that. But your *mammi* will be fine," Lucy said again, praying she was right.

Tamar had closed her eyes now. She was perfectly still as if any movement at all hurt her.

"*Mammi*, can't you get up?" Cornelia asked.

"*Nee*, Nellie," Lucy answered for Tamar. "She's resting. She needs a nap right now."

"But the floor ain't comfortable."

"*Nee*, it ain't. But this is where she needs to stay until your *dat* brings help."

Within fifteen minutes an ambulance came blasting onto the property. Josh pushed through the door ahead of the attendants.

"Right here. She's in here."

The attendants immediately checked Tamar over. After they stabilized her, they carefully lifted her onto the gurney. Lucy's heart was in her throat as she watched Tamar being wheeled out of the house. She put her arms around the children, hugging them to her sides.

"I'm going with her," Josh said, his voice gravelly.

"Of course," Lucy told him. "The *kinner* will be fine with me."

He gave her a grateful nod and hurried out the door behind the gurney. There was sudden silence in the front room, and Lucy felt the children's shock and dismay.

The siren began wailing as the ambulance left, and Cornelia burst into tears.

"It's all right, Nellie. Everything will be all right," Lucy said.

"*Nee*, it ain't!" Cornelia cried. "They took *Mamm* away in an ambulance, too. She never came back."

At her words, David erupted in tears, clenching Lucy's skirt tightly.

"Come on," Lucy said. "Let's make cards for *Mammi*, shall we? Goodness, but she'll like that."

"She ain't coming back," Cornelia sobbed.

"But she is. Come on, Nellie. Let's make cards. We can send them to the hospital with your *dat* later. Your *mammi* won't come home today because she's hurt. But that doesn't mean she won't come home at all."

Cornelia's face had crumpled into a frown, and she wasn't having it. "*Nee*, she ain't coming back."

David was wailing now, and Lucy bent down to pick him up. "Nellie Lambright, you stop talking like that this very minute."

It was the first time Lucy had raised her voice to them, and Cornelia was so surprised, she pressed her lips together in a pout.

"We're not going to talk that way. We're going to make cards for your *mammi*, who is very much alive. And your *dat* will take the cards to her. Now, stop your crying and come on."

Lucy marched over to the bureau with David on her hip. She opened the top drawer where she knew there was paper and crayons. She got them out and carried them to the table. She put David down on the bench and sat beside him.

"You sit on my other side, Nellie. What would you like to draw and color for your *mammi*? What would she like?"

Cornelia gave a big sniff. "She likes sunflowers."

"*Gut*. Then we'll draw sunflowers. What else?"

"She likes me," David said.

Lucy laughed. "That she does. You can draw a picture of yourself."

"She likes me, too," Cornelia said.

"*Jah*, she does. Why don't you draw yourself holding some sunflowers for her?"

"That's hard..."

"Ah, you can do it. I'll help if you need me to."

"What are you gonna draw?" David asked her.

"Hmm." Lucy thought for a moment, doubting seriously Tamar would want anything she drew. "I s'pose I can draw a pretty garden. She'd like that, don't you think?"

David nodded and picked up a brown crayon.

They worked for a good half hour on their pictures. Lucy found herself wishing for one of the *Englischer* cellphones. Then she would know what was happening at the hospital. Her mind was divided between the children and Josh. She prayed all was well and Tamar was all right. She feared the woman had broken her hip, and if so, her recovery would be lengthy.

She and the children made the noon meal. The children were happy to help but when they ate, they grew solemn and kept looking at the spots where their father and grandmother usually sat. Lucy did her best to keep their spirits up, bringing up lively topics to chat about.

"One time, I flew so high in a swing that my *mammi* hollered at me to come back to earth."

"Was it a tire swing?" David asked.

"*Nee*. It was a regular swing. We'd gone to a park in town where they had all sorts of play equipment for *kinner*."

"I ain't never been on a regular swing," Cornelia said.

"Not even at the school?"

"I don't know," Cornelia said and then perked up. "But *Mammi* told me we got a big slide. When I start going to school, I'm gonna go down that slide."

"I wanna go down it," David said.

Cornelia looked at him. "You're too little for school."

"*Nee*, I'm not. I'm big."

"You can't go."

"All right, let's not argue about it," Lucy said. "One of these days, let's walk by the school and see just what they do have."

"Can I come?" David asked.

"Of course, you can come. We'll all go see."

Lucy heard tires crunch in the drive, and she jumped up and ran to the window. A taxi was letting Josh out.

"Your *dat's* back," she cried.

Both children bolted from their seats and ran out of the house. They hardly let Josh take a step before they were in his arms. Lucy hurried to the front porch and stood there, waiting. He looked up at her, and she could see the relief in his eyes.

"How is she?" she asked, amidst the children's questions.

"Let's go inside," Josh said. His voice was tired, but he didn't seem discouraged.

Lucy held the screen door open, and they all went inside to sit in the front room.

"Is she..." Cornelia gulped. "Is she dead?"

"*Ach, nee*," Josh said, grabbing her to him in a hug. "She's hurt, but she's fine. She'll be coming home soon."

"Is it broken?" Lucy asked. "Her hip?"

Josh shook his head. "She's badly bruised, but the x-ray showed no breaks." He shook his head again. "The doctors can't understand it. It should have been broken. They told me that the break often happens before the fall, which seemed odd to me. But they couldn't understand it. They kept saying, 'She's a lucky woman.'"

He laughed outright then. "They kept saying it until *Mamm* snapped, 'Luck don't have nothing to do with it.' *Ach*, but she was annoyed. They'd given her some pain medicine by then, and she was as plucky as ever. In truth, I expected her to come clean out of the bed and give them a lecture or two."

"So, she's coming home?" Cornelia asked. "Truly?"

"Truly," Josh said, smiling warmly at her.

"So, she ain't dead?" David asked, as if he couldn't quite believe it.

"*Nee*, son. She's very much alive."

David looked at Lucy. "Can we have cookie? We didn't get no dessert."

All of them laughed. "I don't see why not," Lucy said, getting up and going to the kitchen.

Josh followed her. "Thank you, Lucy."

She turned to him. "I'm just ever so grateful your *mamm* is all right. How long will she be in the hospital?"

"I can bring her home tomorrow." He frowned slightly. "She's going to need a lot of recovery time. It ain't broke, but she hurt herself badly. I reckon she won't be able to do much for quite a while."

"Don't you worry. I can keep things running."

"Thank you," he said again.

They stood there for a moment, looking at each other, until Lucy felt uncomfortable and turned away. She was apprehensive about the gratitude in his eyes. It made things seem ... well, almost intimate between them, and that simply could not be. She figured she was exaggerating things in her mind, but even so, it was best to step away.

She dug into the cookie jar to pull out three cookies. Since Josh hadn't moved, she asked, "Do you want one?"

He cleared his throat. "Um... Lucy?"

"What?" She felt compelled to look at him again.

"You'll be staying the night with only me and the *kinner*. I know how people's tongues can wag. Are you all right with it? *Mamm* will be home tomorrow." He shifted his weight from one foot to the other.

"You ain't planning anything, are you?" The minute the words escaped her mouth, she nearly died with embarrassment. Why in the world had she said that? Did she think it would be funny? Was she making a joke? And what bad taste...

His eyes widened and then he frowned, studying her. He blinked and then forced a laugh. "I'm sure you're joking. And *nee*, I'm not planning anything."

Her face was on fire. She had never been so ashamed in her life. What had gotten ahold of her?

"I-I'm sorry. J-just a joke."

He gave her a look of compassion then. "That's what I thought. Still, are you all right with it?"

She drew herself up, trying to regain some sense of dignity. "Of course. And Tamar is coming back tomorrow." She inhaled sharply. "Now, are you hungry?"

He raised his brow. "Truth be told, I am."

"I'll get you a plate. Here, would you take the cookies to the *kinner*?"

He took the cookies and nodded. "That I can do."

After he left, she stared at the space where he'd stood. She sighed heavily, feeling like a fool. She'd better watch herself. Clearly, she didn't have total control over herself where Josh was concerned. She shuddered. She couldn't afford to lose focus. She knew what it was like to live with a man; she knew what it was like to lose control over her own life and her own decisions. As an Amish woman, she also knew what men expected.

At least, she knew what her father expected, and it was complete obedience and loyalty. Even when it hurt. She clasped her hands together and rocked on her feet. She couldn't do it. Not again. She wanted to be free of men. She wanted to be in charge of her own life.

Was that wrong? Was God not pleased with her opinion or thoughts?

She walked to the fridge to take out the leftovers. Best to avoid the entire subject by keeping her distance. Besides, Josh was a new widower; she was foolish to think he'd ever be interested in her, anyway.

# Chapter Thirteen

Josh sat on the davenport and stretched out his legs. He was tired. It had been a trying day, what with his mother getting hurt. But now, he'd seen to the animals, and Lucy had prepared a hearty plate of food for him. It was odd to eat with the plate balanced in his hands as he sat on the couch. In truth, he couldn't remember another time he'd eaten so.

But this evening, well, he just couldn't bring up the energy to move. And Lucy had brought him his plate and all. The *kinner* were upstairs playing quietly—which was a miracle in itself.

And speaking of miracles, he was deeply grateful to God for his mother's welfare. How she'd escaped a broken hip boggled his mind, too. He supposed that beneath her weakness of late, she was still the tough, wiry woman he remembered.

In any case, he was relieved.

He glanced toward the door of the room. He could hear Lucy in the kitchen, setting things to right. It was a good thing she was there. With her injury, his mother would be completely incapable of running the household and watching his *kinner*. And Lucy seemed willing to take it all on.

*Ach*, but that was an awkward moment earlier. She had clearly spoken without thinking. Still, it was a mighty odd thing to say. Once again, he wondered at her past. What had happened to her? And to say such a thing ... it made him wonder if she'd been hurt somehow.

That would also explain why she hadn't married. Truth was, Lucy was somewhat of a puzzle to him. He chuckled slightly, remembering the look of horror on her face when she realized what she had said—what she had implied. It wasn't funny; even now, it wasn't funny. But goodness, that look on her face. She would have disappeared in front of him if she'd been able.

She was a funny one, for sure and for certain. He felt an urge to get to know her better, but he stifled the urge just as quickly. *Ach*, he didn't need to know her to have her work for him. He only had to know she was a good person, and that he already inherently knew.

His children were growing fond of her. Cornelia was smitten, and that was no easy thing.

"Do you need anything else?" Lucy asked him from the doorway.

He gave a start and sat up a bit straighter.

"You must think me awful for eating in here like this," he said, smiling.

"*Nee*. It's been a hard day."

"That it has. I hope *Mamm* passes a *gut* night."

"I think they'll make sure she sleeps," Lucy said, clearly knowing the *Englisch* had medicine for everything.

He nodded and toyed with his fork for a minute. "You must be tired, too."

"*Ach*, I'm fine."

"Why don't you come in and sit a spell?" He nearly dropped his plate. Why had he suggested that?

She quickly shook her head. "I need to go check on the *kinner*."

And with that, she hurried away.

Well, now he'd done it. Scared her off. She'd think he had something planned, after all. He burst into laughter. What a thought. And what a day.

Tomorrow couldn't come soon enough.

The next morning, Bartholomew got into the van he'd hired to take him to Hollybrook. He had a plan. He was going to locate Lucy—which should be easy enough if he checked with the local mercantile. They would tell him where she was and what family she was helping. Then he would go to wherever Lucy was and demand she come home.

"Good morning," the driver greeted him as he settled into the backseat.

"Morning," Bartholomew grumbled. "You remember I want a ride home, too?"

"Yes, you told me."

"I don't know how long you'll have to wait. It shouldn't be long."

"It's fine. I've got all day."

"Won't take all day."

The driver shrugged and put the car into gear. He rolled down the driveway and onto the road. Bartholomew's stomach was none too happy. *Ach*, was he nervous? Why should he be? He was only going to bring his own daughter back home. Nothing to be nervous about there. He was completely in the right. But nevertheless, he was nervous. And that made him angry.

He shifted and stared out the side window.

During the entire ride, he barely moved. The driver tried a couple times to engage him in conversation, but it was fruitless. Bartholomew was distracted, and he aimed to stay that way.

"Take me to the local mercantile," he finally spoke when they passed the sign welcoming them to Hollybrook, Indiana.

"That'd be the Feed & Supply," the driver said. "I know it."

Bartholomew grunted and folded his arms across his chest. Within minutes, the driver turned into the parking lot and cut the engine.

"I'll be right back," Bartholomew said, climbing out of the van. He heard the driver get out behind him and turned to see him stretching but staying by his open door.

The bell above the door tinkled as Bartholomew walked inside. A pudgy woman behind the counter looked over at him.

"Welcome to the Feed & Supply. I don't believe you're from around here."

Bartholomew gave her a smile. Just as he thought, whoever worked at the local mercantile in an Amish community would know everyone and everything. He walked to the counter.

"You're right at that," he said, infusing his voice with friendliness. "Name is Bartholomew Oyer."

"I'm Eliza Troyer. How can I help you?"

Bartholomew figured she'd become even more loose-lipped if he bought something. He picked up an apple from the basket on the counter.

"I'll take this apple and … a carton of juice." He pointed to the cooler. "Orange juice."

Eliza grinned and went to the cooler and took out her largest carton of orange juice. "Anything else?"

She punched in the numbers into her old-fashioned cash register.

"*Nee*, that will do it." He paid her and then made to leave, pausing and turning back, as if it were an afterthought.

"I hear Lucy Oyer moved to the area recently. Can you tell me where to find her?"

Eliza's brow rose. "You kin?"

"*Jah*. Not close, though." How could he admit he didn't know the whereabouts of his own daughter?

"She's watching the Lambright *kinner*. Poor Josh. My heart goes out to the lad. Losing his wife and then his *dat*. Has to be hard." She tsk-ed her tongue and shook her head.

"*Jah*. Has to be," Bartholomew agreed, putting on a sympathetic face. "Well, thanks for the apple and juice. I'll be seeing you."

Her brow rose higher at that. "Oh, are you staying in the—"

But he didn't stick around to hear the rest of her question or to answer her. She was a busy-body, pure and simple. And while he was happy to take advantage of it, he wasn't eager to give her more cud to chew on. He walked to the van and climbed in.

"We need to go to the Lambrights."

The driver scowled. "I'm going to need more than that. I don't know where everyone around here lives."

Bartholomew inhaled sharply. Why in the world hadn't he asked for directions?

"Uh…" He rolled down his window and leaned out, calling out to a customer who had just arrived. "Hello there," he said. "Can you direct me to the Lambright farm?"

The man smiled and sauntered over to the van. "I could. They ain't that far from here. You got business there?"

"Just visiting, and I forgot the location."

"Go on down the road a piece until you hit a fork. Take the right and it's … uh … the fourth farm down on the right-hand side of the road."

"Thank you."

"I'm glad to meet you. Amos Byler is the na—"

But Bartholomew had already rolled his window back up. He gave a short wave to the surprised and somewhat offended-looking man.

"You heard him?" Bartholomew asked the driver.

"I heard him." And he started up the engine and pulled out of the parking lot. "You want me to sit at the farm and wait for you?"

Bartholomew considered this. He hadn't thought that part through. He supposed it wouldn't hurt any. The driver could park the van under a tree somewhere and wait.

"*Jah.* That's likely what we'll do. As I said, it won't take long."

They went on down the road, following the stranger's directions. When the driver pulled into the fourth farm on the right, Bartholomew felt sweaty.

"Here we are," the driver announced.

"I can see that."

The driver pointed to a shady spot to park. "I'll be waiting over there."

"Fine." Bartholomew straightened his spine and climbed out of the van.

# Chapter Fourteen

"Someone's here," Cornelia announced to Lucy. "It's a van."

"*Ach,* maybe your *dat* has returned with your *mammi*," Lucy said, hurrying to the front door. She had already made up the davenport into a bed for the older woman. She'd also arranged a small table to set beside it. There was a glass of water waiting there, along with a napkin and the latest Amish newspaper she'd found on the bureau. She wondered how Tamar would be. She would have to still be in pain, for sure and for certain.

She pulled open the door and froze. Her heart lurched. "D-Dat? What are you doing here?"

Bartholomew yanked the screen door open and pushed his way inside.

"Who are you?" Cornelia asked. "Where's *Mammi*?"

Bartholomew frowned down at her. "I don't know where your *mammi* is."

"Hi, *Mammi*," David cried rushing into the entry way. He stopped short and gawked. "You ain't my *mammi*. Where's *Dat*?"

"I don't know," snapped Bartholomew. He looked at Lucy. "Gather your things."

"What?"

"You're coming home with me. The van is waiting outside."

Lucy nearly choked with indignation. "I'm not going with you. I have a job. And these *kinner* are alone. I'm watching them."

"Well, someone else is going to have to do it. You need to come with me."

Lucy's jaw tightened. She turned to the children. "You two go on out and play now. I'll be out soon to push you in the swing."

Cornelia looked doubtful. David turned and ran.

"Go on now, Nellie."

"Who is he?"

"He's my *dat*. It's fine. Run along and play now."

But Cornelia didn't move an inch.

137

"You heard her," Bartholomew said. "Go outside."

Cornelia's mouth tightened. "You can't take her away. *Dat* said she's staying."

"I'm her *dat*," Bartholomew said. "What I say, goes."

"Outside," Lucy said, widening her eyes at Cornelia. "Everything is fine. I'll be out in a few minutes."

"But—"

"Go on" Lucy said. Finally, Cornelia obeyed, looking very upset about it.

"See?" Bartholomew said. "They don't even obey you. Now run along and get your things."

"I'm not going." Lucy stretched up to her full height.

"I'm your father. It's my *Gott*-given right to make decisions for you."

"*Jah*, when I was a child. I'm all grown up now."

"Don't make no difference. You ain't married."

Lucy fumed. "And I ain't going to be married. So get used to that idea, too. You've wasted your money on this trip, *Dat*. I'm not going."

Her father looked momentarily bewildered. But then, his face hardened. "I'll wait for you here."

He marched into the front room and glanced about, seeing the bed on the davenport. "Is this where they have you sleeping? In the front room? What kind of—"

"That bed is for Tamar, the *kinner's mammi*. She fell and hurt herself and is coming home from the hospital today. She can't be climbing the steps to her bedroom."

Bartholomew snorted. "So they're needing a nurse or something."

"*Nee.* They need me," Lucy said feeling the truth of it. She knew her father needed her, too, but somehow it felt different knowing the children and Josh needed her. And Tamar needed her to, whether the woman would admit it or not. Lucy realized again there was no place else she'd rather be than right here with this family.

Bartholomew sat down in a rocker and didn't speak for a moment. Finally, he said, "You can't be ignoring your *Gott*-given responsibilities. And those are at home, where you belong."

He'd changed course now. He'd softened his voice to appeal to her guilt. And in truth, she did feel guilty for leaving him, but her reasons for leaving were so overpowering that she simply couldn't—wouldn't—give in to that guilt.

She sank down on the rocker beside his. "You can get someone in. I've thought of some wonderful women who could help with the cooking and the cleaning. It would just be a day job—wouldn't even have to be full-time. I have the list. I was going to write—"

"A list? You're replacing yourself with a list? You're my own daughter—my flesh and blood. Your place is with me. What would your *mamm* think of you? She'd be right disappointed, she would."

His voice grew louder as he spoke.

"Don't bring *Mamm* into this."

"And why not? She'd be ashamed of you. Leaving your home."

Visions of her mother's kind face flashed through Lucy's mind. Visions of her mother teaching her how to run a household. Visions of her mother laughing uproariously at something Lucy had said.

"*Nee*," she said softly, shaking her head. "*Nee*, she wouldn't be ashamed."

Bartholomew jumped out of his chair at that. "She would! I knew her better than anyone else. Now, get your things."

"I'm not going. Are you going to hit me now?" As soon as the words left her mouth, Lucy gasped. She had never, never, *never* been so daring as to say something like that. Instinctively, she cowered back in her chair.

Her father froze with his hands fisted at his sides. He glared at her, breathing hard. And then came the sound of another set of wheels crunching in the drive. Her father blinked and turned his head toward the door.

Lucy jumped to her feet and hurried past him. She felt sick—completely sick as if she could vomit. How had things deteriorated so badly that she would fling such accusations at her father, or that he'd have his fists ready as if just waiting for an excuse to use them?

He wouldn't use them. No. He wouldn't. Not here. He'd been rough with her before, pushing her, knocking into her, and yes, hitting her. But he wouldn't have used his fists on her—he wouldn't. He would have stopped himself.

Wouldn't he?

She swallowed hard and opened the door. There was Josh, climbing out of the van.

"*Ach*, Lucy, we're home," he told her. He glanced at the van parked under the trees. "Who's here?"

Lucy hurried down the steps. "How is your mother?" she asked, ignoring his question.

The two children came running, jumping up and down in their excitement.

"She's home," Cornelia cried. She looked at Lucy with tears in her eyes. "She came home, just like you said."

Lucy nodded; too much emotion was sweeping through her. She daren't look back toward the house. She didn't want to see her father staring at them. She didn't want to see her father at all. Had he stayed back in the house? Was he indeed on the porch looking at them?

"Stay back, *kinner*, give your *mammi* room to breathe."

He'd opened the back sliding door of the van. Tamar was leaning against the seat, half sitting, half lying.

"I have room to breathe," she said crossly.

"How do we help her inside?" Lucy asked, stepping closer to the van.

"I'm going to carry her. I think it'll be easier."

"You ain't carrying me into my own house," Tamar snapped. "Back up, the both of you."

Lucy stepped back, but Josh remained where he was. "I ain't arguing with you, *Mamm*. And if you're going to be cranky and stubborn, I'm taking you back to the hospital. Now, let me pick you up while your pain medication is still working."

Tamar pursed her lips, but she didn't argue further. Josh, ever-so-carefully, stepped inside the van and slipped his arms beneath her. Lucy couldn't help but notice the way his muscles bulged as he took his mother in his arms and maneuvered her out of the van.

He tipped his head toward the driver. "Thank you. I'll call if we need you again."

Lucy pushed the van door closed, and the van pulled away.

"Now, let's get you inside," Josh said gently to his mother, who had closed her eyes. Her face indicated discomfort, but the pain medication must have still been working, for she didn't look too strained.

Josh looked at Lucy. "Who's here?"

The screen door opened, and Bartholomew stepped out onto the porch. Josh's brow furrowed. "Hello? Who are you?"

Tamar opened her eyes, and looked at Lucy's father, but then she closed them again.

"I'm Lucy's *dat*," he said, his voice heavy. "As soon as you're able, I need to talk to you."

Josh gave Lucy a confused look, but he was clearly more focused on getting his mother settled.

"I've made up a bed for her in the front room," Lucy said, scurrying to keep up. "I thought it'd be easier than taking her upstairs."

"*Gut* idea. Thank you."

Tamar's eyes flew open at that. "I ain't sleeping in the front room. Take me to my bedroom."

"*Nee, Mamm.* Lucy's right. You don't need to be climbing stairs."

"I'll stay put up there."

"You'd be lonely. This is better," Josh insisted. He carefully lowered her to the davenport.

Tamar let out an involuntary moan and then clamped her lips together in a tight line.

"There's some water for you, and if you need anything else, you just ask," Lucy said.

She expected Tamar to bite her head off, but to her surprise, the woman merely nodded, and if Lucy wasn't mistaken, she appeared a bit grateful, although the look was fleeting.

"You all right now?" Josh turned to address the children. "You two can visit with your *mammi* unless she's tired. There will be no sitting on the davenport by her. You can sit on the floor. I'm serious now. No sitting on the davenport. *Mammi's* hip has to heal."

"Does she have medicine?" Lucy asked, doing her best to ignore her father's looming presence behind them.

"She does. But she doesn't take the next dose for a few more hours."

"Quit babbling about me as if I'm not here," Tamar said, but then she fell back onto the pillow as if the exertion of speaking was too much.

"*Kinner*," Lucy said quietly, "why don't you go back out and play for a while now? You can see your *mammi* later."

Cornelia didn't look any too pleased, but she grabbed David's hand and started to leave the room, only to stop before Bartholomew and stare at him. She opened her mouth as if to say something and Lucy's breath caught. But thankfully, she didn't make any comment. She just tugged on her brother, and they both left.

"Now," Josh said, straightening up and facing Bartholomew. "So you're Lucy's *dat*. Welcome to our home—"

"We need to talk," Bartholomew said. He glanced at Tamar. "Let's go out to the porch."

Josh looked at Lucy and then nodded. "That's fine. Lucy, can you bring some lemonade out?"

"I... I'd rather come with you outside now."

Josh frowned, but he didn't argue. The three of them went out to the porch.

"Is something troubling you?" Josh asked. "I assure you Lucy is fine. We've been right grateful to have her here."

"She needs to come home with me. *Now*."

"*Dat*—"

Bartholomew gave her a look of warning.

Josh looked back and forth between the two. "I don't understand," he said finally.

"She needs to be at home. She has a job looking after the house and the garden. She just up and left without my permission."

Lucy wished the porch would open up and swallow her. This was beyond embarrassing. She felt like a young child being scolded by her father.

"But..." Josh sighed heavily. "We need her more than ever here. You can see my *mamm* has been injured. I have two *kinner*, and they need tending. I'm busy out in the fields—"

Bartholomew shook his head. "Don't matter. She never should have left. You can get someone else in."

"So can you," Lucy blurted. Her face went hot. *Ach*, what must Josh think of her? She was being downright sassy to her own father.

"Enough," Bartholomew said harshly. "I didn't come to discuss this. I came to fetch my daughter. I'm just informing you."

Lucy's heart was racing wildly. If she didn't handle this, she'd be forced to return home—and she didn't want to go. She didn't want to leave Cornelia and David ... and Josh. Even Tamar. She was making progress with the woman, and it was so gratifying. *Ach*, but she was considering this her home now.

"I'm not going," she said quietly. Both men turned to stare at her.

"*Jah*, you are."

"*Nee*, I'm not. I'll go get the lemonade now, Josh."

Josh's eyes were wide, and there was something in his look. She didn't dare stand there long enough to figure out what it was. Because if it was shock or shame or censure, she didn't want to know.

She turned on her heel and left the porch, her heart now hammering inside her. What would happen? Her father couldn't physically force her into the van, could he? Josh wouldn't let him, would he?

She blinked back hot tears and walked to the kitchen. She worked as slowly as she dared, pouring lemonade into three glasses, even though she knew her father wouldn't drink a drop of it. He was furious with her, and he wasn't used to being defied—especially in front of others. She grasped the counter and held on, knowing she didn't have the courage to go out there again and face him.

Better to stay right there, in the kitchen. Better not to move. Better not to know…

She stood there a full two minutes until she heard an engine cough to life. She flew to the window and looked out. The van —her father's hired van—was leaving. She could make out the silhouette of her father in the back seat. She held her breath until the van disappeared out onto the road, and then she nearly collapsed with relief.

She made her way to the kitchen bench and sank onto it, suddenly dizzy.

And then she heard footsteps and Josh was there, in the kitchen, and she could feel him staring at her. She looked up, into his eyes, meeting his look of both pity and pride. She blinked, and swallowed the vomit that was creeping up her throat.

"He says it ain't over," Josh said softly.

She swallowed again. "I'm sure it ain't."

He came over to stand in front of her, his large frame both encompassing and unnerving. "I'm sorry."

She blinked up at him. "It... It isn't your fault."

He lowered himself to the bench beside her. "*Nee*. But still, I'm sorry."

Her breath seeped out of her. She had a sudden, inexplicable urge to fall against him and let him comfort her. She was so stunned by it that she leaned away from him. He didn't seem to notice. Instead, he placed his hand softly her shoulder, and it was as if his touch burned into her, sinking down to her toes. She gasped, and he dropped his hand.

Neither of them spoke for a long moment. The ticking of the clock over the stove sounded like loud gongs in the silence. Sounds of the children playing wafted faintly through the window.

"Has he ... has he hurt you?" Josh finally asked.

She blinked rapidly. "I s'pose—I s'pose it depends on what you mean by hurt."

Josh sucked in his breath and looked away. She saw his jaw tighten.

"You don't have to go back," he said.

She took a breath.

"But he'll return," she whispered.

Josh shrugged. "I'll be here to meet him."

Her forehead crinkled. "What... What do you mean?"

He looked at her, his eyes boring into hers. "I mean, I'll be here. You don't have to go back."

Tears flooded her eyes, and she looked away, embarrassed to be crying. No man had ever—*ever*...

Ever what? Defended her? Listened to her? Considered her feelings?

She wiped impatiently at her tears. "I have the lemonade poured," she said.

Such a ridiculous comment. So out of place. So normal. Absurd, really, and they both knew it. He started laughing first, and then she joined him. She felt the tension leave her. She knew the relief was temporary, for she knew her father would be back. He wouldn't take it lightly that he had been crossed—and in front of strangers.

But for now, this minute, she felt better; lighter than she'd felt in years. And the fact that she was sharing this moment with a man wasn't lost on her.

## Chapter Fifteen

Josh gritted his teeth and shoveled the manure with abrupt jerky motions. He didn't know when he'd been so vexed. That father of Lucy was something else. He'd feared for a minute or two the man wasn't going to leave the day before. Finally in exasperation, he had stomped off and climbed into his hired van. Good thing, too, for Josh had been about to grab the man's arm and guide him forcefully to the van if he hadn't moved.

Well, Josh had been wondering what there was about Lucy—why she hadn't married, why she didn't already have a passel of children, why she'd been so eager to leave home and move to another district to take care of his children.

Now he knew.

Or he thought he did. What woman would be eager to marry when her primary example of a man was someone like Bartholomew Oyer?

He shoveled another pitchfork of hay and manure into the waiting wheelbarrow. At least Lucy was out from under her father's roof now. She would be happier here with his family—or so he hoped. He felt determined to make sure she was. *Ach*, but it wasn't really his business, was it? Still, he felt the desire harden within him.

No one should have to put up with that kind of treatment. Least of all Lucy. She was so sweet and capable and hard-working. He watched how she poured out her love to his children. And even the way she treated his mother. She was special.

He thought again of the harsh look on Bartholomew's face when he'd ordered Lucy to go with him. Josh understood as well as any Amish man, the role of the father over his daughters. He understood the authority it carried.

But in this case? It wasn't right. And Lucy was hardly a child anymore.

No, Lucy had been right to leave her father. *Ach*, but he'd wanted to put his arms around her last night and comfort her. The desire had caught him off guard, and it had bothered him greatly. Not only at the moment, but later, when he was in bed thinking about it. He wasn't in the habit of comforting women with an embrace, and he wasn't about to start now. Goodness, but what would she have thought?

Anyway, it was just sympathy. Yes. Just sympathy and compassion.

He turned again to mucking out the stall. He had a lot to do that day. Best he keep his mind on it.

~

Lucy took the broom into the front room and hesitated. Tamar had her eyes closed, and Lucy didn't want to disturb her by sweeping the room. After all, the front room was basically Tamar's bedroom right now.

She turned quietly to go but was stopped when Tamar spoke.

"Go ahead," she said. "Go ahead and sweep. I'm awake."

Lucy turned back around. "If you're sure."

"I said so, didn't I?"

Lucy smiled. In truth, she was happy to hear Tamar's snippy answer. It meant she must be feeling stronger and more like herself. Lucy began to sweep, being careful to reach into the corners and under the furniture as best she could without moving it all about.

"Sit down," Tamar said when Lucy was done.

Surprised, Lucy paused and sat on the chair closest to the davenport. "Is there something you need?"

"I heard."

"Heard what?"

Tamar made a face. "I heard your *dat* out on the porch yesterday. He wants you to leave."

"That he does." Lucy inhaled deeply, waiting for Tamar to scold her for not going—not obeying.

"He always that harsh?" Tamar continued.

Lucy's brow rose. "What? Um. Mostly."

Tamar pursed her lips and nodded. "I see."

Lucy waited. Was there something else Tamar wanted to say? She was frowning now, and she was rubbing her hip.

Lucy jumped up. "Are you in pain again? Do you need another pill?"

Tamar swiped her arm through the air impatiently. "Sit down."

Lucy did.

"My pain ain't your concern."

"But if I can help—"

"Goodness, child. You talk too much."

Lucy clamped her mouth closed, but not before thinking how Cornelia had her completely beat in the talking department. She stifled a smile at the thought.

"Sorry," Lucy told her.

Tamar scowled. "You were right."

"What?"

"You were right to leave him."

Lucy's eyes widened. She would never have thought to hear Tamar say such a thing. She figured Tamar was likely as strict as they came when discussing the chain of authority in Amish families.

"He is my father..."

"Of course, he is, and I s'pose we can't be questioning *Gott* about that. And don't look so surprised. Despite your opinion, I'm not some kind of monster."

"But I never sai—"

"Pshaw, child. You didn't have to say a word. I can see, can't I? Despite what my son thinks, I ain't dead yet."

"But Josh doesn't—"

"Goodness, there you go again. You talk too much."

Again, Lucy clamped her mouth shut and went completely still.

"I'm an old woman, and I know how things work. You ain't married, so you should still be under your father's authority. But sometimes, well..." She paused and sniffed and shook her head slowly. "I've seen a lot of things in my day. And unfortunately, I haven't liked some of them. When things are taken too far—" Her eyes drilled into Lucy's "—And *everything* can be taken too far—bad things can happen."

Lucy knew better than to question her or to say a word.

"I've seen some awful things happen because the man was given too much power." Her eyes narrowed. "Now, don't get me wrong, girl. I do believe the man is the head of the household. But if he's ... cruel ... if he's ... mean ... well, I can't believe *Gott* is approving of that."

Lucy blinked at her. Not many Amish women she knew would agree—or at least admit to it out loud.

"So, you done right in leaving."

Lucy's throat tightened, and she felt tears near the surface. She was overcome with a sudden rush of love for this cantankerous woman.

Tamar laughed, and then winced as if in pain. "You got an open face. I can see your thoughts rolling around. You're surprised that a mean old woman like me could be understanding."

"It's not that..."

"*Jah*, it is that. And it's my fault, I s'pose." She shook her head. "Now, don't go thinking I'm going to be all nice to you now."

Lucy couldn't help but laugh. "I wouldn't dare think such a thing."

Tamar raised her chin. "*Gut*. As long as we understand each other."

Lucy stood up and dared take a step nearer. She leaned down and despite Tamar's instant recoiling, she kissed the top of her *kapp*.

"Just so there's no misunderstanding," Lucy murmured, smiling gently.

"*Ach*, go finish your cleaning."

Lucy turned and picked up her broom which was lying against the arm of the chair. "I'll send Cornelia in," she said, mischievously. "If you think *I* talk too much—"

She left the sentence hanging and left the room, but behind her, she heard Tamar chuckling.

# Chapter Sixteen

Two weeks later, when Lucy was in the kitchen kneading enough bread dough to make four loaves, she heard someone at the front door. Goodness, but had someone driven up in a buggy and she hadn't heard it?

"Lucy," Cornelia hollered from the entry way. "Someone's here."

Lucy quickly rinsed her hands, grabbed a dishtowel, and hurried to the front door. Cornelia had disappeared outside. On the doorstep stood a woman who was likely in her twenties, holding a casserole dish.

"*Ach*, who are you?" the woman asked, her brown eyes filled with curiosity.

"I'm Lucy Oyer," Lucy said, her eyes narrowing slightly. Lucy knew when she was being assessed. Instinctively, she stood a little straighter.

"I... I, uh, well, is Tamar's... I mean, is Josh Lambright in?"

"He's working in the fields. Can I help you?"

"Are you kin?"

"*Nee.* I'm here helping out." For some reason, Lucy took an instant dislike to the woman. There was no reason to, either, for she appeared nice enough.

"I'd hoped to see Josh."

Lucy stared at the casserole in the woman's hands. "Is that for the family?"

"*Ach, jah,*" the woman said, blinking as if she were surprised to find it in her own hands. "I heard Tamar had fallen. And I figured Josh would be glad for some help."

"I'm sure he'll appreciate the casserole." She reached out to take it, but the woman held on. Lucy went on, "Um, who should I say brought it?"

"Glenda. Glenda Zook."

"He'll be right thankful. Would you... Would you like to come in and see Tamar?"

Glenda bit the side of her lip. "I wouldn't want to bother her."

159

"It'd be no bother."

But still, Glenda looked hesitant. "I think I'll stop by later, maybe. I just wanted to get the casserole to Josh. You'll tell him, won't you?"

"Of course. Glenda Zook. I won't forget."

Glenda smiled, and Lucy had to admit she was quite pretty, which for some reason, she found annoying.

"Thank you." Glenda stood for another second or two and then nodded. "I'll be going."

"It was nice to meet you." Lucy shifted to see beyond Glenda out to the yard. "Did you drive a buggy?"

"I had my brother bring me, and he dropped me at the end of the drive. I'll walk home."

"I can give you a ride. It wouldn't take long to hitch up the pony cart."

"*Nee.* It ain't so far." Now she seemed in a hurry to leave. With one last scrutinizing glance at Lucy, she was off, waving at the children who were climbing the oak tree which held the tire swing.

Lucy watched her go. The children jumped down from the fairly low branch they were on and came running.

"What'd she want?" Cornelia asked.

"She brought us dinner," Lucy said, holding up the casserole. "Did you children feed the chickens this morning?"

"A long time ago," David told her.

"And you've brushed your teeth?"

Cornelia groaned. "You already asked us that this morning."

Lucy laughed. "So I did. All right then, go on and keep playing."

She went inside, the screen door banging shut behind her.

"Who was that?" Tamar called from the front room.

Lucy went to the doorway. "That was Glenda Zook. She brought a casserole."

"She couldn't be bothered to say hello?"

Lucy shrugged. "She just seemed keen to let Josh know it was she who brought the food."

Tamar scowled. "I see. Well, it didn't take long, did it?"

"What didn't?"

"For the women to start..." She shook her head and closed her eyes as if going to sleep.

Lucy waited a beat and then took the casserole to the kitchen. She knew exactly what Tamar meant; hadn't she thought the same thing herself? The single women were beginning to circle. She inhaled sharply. Glenda Zook was pretty and clearly available. Would Josh be interested?

And what if he was? She blew out her breath. It could mean her job could be over much more quickly than she wanted. And that was the only reason she should be upset if Josh wanted to court someone. The only reason.

She took the casserole into the kitchen and plunked it onto the counter. She peeled back the tinfoil and saw that it was mainly potatoes and carrots with chunks of beef. The sauce looked to have some cheese in it. Truly, it smelled delicious. She grimaced and stuck her little finger into the sauce, licking it off. Just as delicious as it looked. Well, if Josh went for Glenda, he'd be well fed.

She turned back to her dough and punched it down somewhat vigorously. She wondered if she could conveniently forget Glenda's name. The idea made her laugh. She wouldn't dare.

An hour later, the bread was fully risen and ready to be baked. She put the pans into the oven and then put together a salad to be served with the casserole. She had already warmed it up before putting the bread in the oven, so the noon meal was about ready.

Cornelia and David were setting the table for her.

"Go and see if your *mammi* would like to come to the table," she told Cornelia. "If she doesn't, I'll be happy to fix her a plate and take it in."

Tamar had only been to the table once since getting home, and Lucy was trying to get her up and moving a bit more these days. She knew that ideally, Tamar would probably be getting special exercises from the *Englisch* doctors, but Tamar was vehemently opposed to it, so Lucy did her best with keeping her moving as much as she could without overdoing it.

Josh appreciated her efforts with his mother, which made Lucy feel warm all over. She liked being appreciated. At times, she wondered if she was becoming selfish or vain because she liked compliments so much, but she couldn't seem to help herself.

Still, she and Josh didn't talk too much together. Ever since her father had come, and Josh had been so good about it, Lucy had tried to keep her distance. She feared becoming dependent on Josh somehow. But now, as she thought about him possibly chatting with Glenda, it irked her. If he chatted with anyone, it should be her, shouldn't it?

"*Ach*, Lucy," she muttered to herself. "You can't have it both ways, you know."

"*Mammi* wants to come to the table," Cornelia announced, coming into the kitchen.

"Thank you. I'll help her. Can you take the pitcher of milk? It's right heavy you know."

"I can do it."

"I wanna carry it," David complained. "I'm big now."

"That you are," Lucy said. "How about you carry the big serving spoon and fork for the salad? And you can carry the bottle of dressing, too."

He grinned at that, content. The side door opened and slammed shut. Josh came into the kitchen. "What smells so *gut?*"

Lucy smiled. "The noon meal. Go on and wash up. I'm going to help your *mamm* to the table."

Josh looked pleased. "She's joining us?"

"That she is."

"Let me help her. Give me a moment to wash up."

"All right." Lucy picked up the casserole using hot pads and carried it to the dining table. She went back for the salad. The children had done their toting and had sat down in their spots. Josh had washed and was now bringing his mother in. Tamar leaned heavily against him, but her face wasn't contorted as it sometimes was when she was up and walking.

"Here you go, *Mamm*," Josh said, lowering his mother onto the chair at the end of the table.

Josh then sat down, and so did Lucy.

"Shall we have our silent blessing?" Josh asked. He bowed his head. Lucy bowed her head and closed her eyes. She thanked

*Gott* for the food, even though she had mixed feelings about it. When Josh cleared his throat, they all looked up.

"I'm hungry," Cornelia said.

"You're always hungry," Josh commented, grinning.

He and Lucy proceeded to dish up food for the children. Lucy helped with Tamar's plate, grateful she didn't fuss about it. When everyone was served and had begun to eat, Tamar gave a little cough and looked at Josh.

"Did Lucy tell you who made the casserole?"

Josh smiled. "I assume she did."

"You'd be assuming wrong."

He raised a brow. "Don't tell me Cornelia made it?"

Cornelia giggled. "I can't do that. It was that woman."

"That woman?"

"*Jah*. Some woman came over."

Josh gave Lucy a perplexed look. Lucy carefully put on a smile. "Glenda Zook made the casserole for you, and she brought it over earlier today."

"This woman made it for me?" Josh asked, and then he laughed. "So, none of you should be eating any then?"

"*Dat*," David cried with his mouth full. "We're hungry, too."

Josh looked at his mother. "Glenda Zook? Who is she?"

Tamar shrugged. "Someone who wants courting."

Lucy had been drinking her milk, and she nearly spit it out over all her food. Tamar was going to be as frank as that?

Josh looked as if he would have spit out his milk out too, had he been drinking any.

"Wh-what?" he asked.

"You heard me, son. She's fixing to get noticed, and cooking is as *gut* a way as any."

Josh was staring at his mother. "Get noticed?"

"*Ach*, son, you can't be as ignorant as that. You know all the single women will be looking your way."

Cornelia's face had scrunched up in a frown. "What for? Why are they looking? And what's courting?"

"Don't you pay any—" Josh started, but Tamar interrupted him.

"They'll be looking to marry your *dat*."

Cornelia looked horrified. "Why?"

Tamar shrugged. "They just are."

"*Mamm*, do you have to go on about it?" Josh asked, his face flushed.

"Might as well face facts, son. I reckon we'll be getting quite a few casseroles now. Once word is out that Glenda has started the ball rolling so to speak."

Lucy watched Josh's face register dread, and she was glad for it. Good. So, he wasn't looking for someone to court.

"Marry him?" Cornelia sputtered. "He don't have to." She looked directly at Lucy. "He can marry Lucy. Then she can stay forever."

Lucy sucked in her breath. *Ach,* but the child never stopped talking. Except now, a silence fell over the table. She stared down at her plate afraid to look up, afraid she'd see that same look of dread on Josh's face.

Tamar cleared her throat. "Ain't the worst idea," she said. Her voice was low, but everyone could hear her.

Lucy's glaze darted to her. What? Was she actually condoning her and Josh? Tamar—who only recently was beginning to thaw toward her?

Josh stood up, his chair screeching behind him. Then Lucy did look at him, but he wasn't looking at her. He wasn't looking at anyone.

"I think..." he started. "I think I forgot to latch the horse's stall door." And with that, he fled from the room.

Lucy's face went hot. So, the very idea of marrying her sent him running. Though she had no intention of marrying, humiliation swept through her, and she had to resist the urge to go running from the room herself. Only Tamar seemed completely calm.

"Pass me the salad, would you, Cornelia?"

Cornelia pushed the bowl of salad toward her grandmother. Lucy could tell Cornelia was primed to blurt out something else, but shockingly, she remained silent and simply ate her diner. The rest of them did the same, although Lucy had a great deal of trouble swallowing. Goodness, but this meal couldn't be over soon enough.

After getting Tamar back to her bed on the davenport, Lucy cleared the table, did the dishes and *redded* up the kitchen. The children were happily occupied with crayons and coloring books on the front porch. Lucy took the opportunity to get outside by herself for a moment. She figured Josh would be back out in the fields even though he didn't have any meal to speak of. And she didn't want to sit on the front porch with the children right then. So she walked back toward the chicken coop, figuring she could watch them flutter around, pecking the dirt for any errant seed. She enjoyed the chickens. Enjoyed their silly, jerky movements and their social chattering.

She gripped the mesh fence and leaned forward. "Hello, chickies," she said softly. "What are you all taking about today? It's going to be a hot one, you know. Before long, you'll likely all escape back into your nesting boxes."

One hen stopped her pecking and cast her beady eyes on Lucy. The creature tipped her head as if listening intently and understanding every word. Lucy began to laugh.

"What's so funny?"

Lucy jumped and swirled around to see Josh right behind her.

"*Ach*, I didn't hear you," she cried.

"Sorry about that."

She shook her head, "No harm done." She felt completely uncomfortable with him so close, especially on the heels of his disappearance during the noon meal. Why was he with her now, anyway? Did he want to tell her again about how he had no interest in marrying her?

And what was wrong with her anyway that he'd have such a huge reaction? She flinched. *Ach*, but where was her mind going?

"I-I wanted to … apologize," Josh said, his voice faltering.

"Apologize?" she asked, though she knew why.

"I didn't mean to…" He sighed. "It all took me by surprise. I don't even know this Glenda person. And then, *Mamm's* comments…"

She gave him what she hoped was a completely neutral, unemotional look. "Don't give it another thought."

"But I fear I was rude, and I wanted to make sure—"

"You weren't rude," she told him, even though he had been. "You were simply making your feelings known."

He frowned. "*Nee*, that's not what I meant. I mean, like I said, it all took me by surprise. And then when Cornelia blurted out her thoughts, I just... I couldn't stay."

Lucy worked to keep her expression in place. "It doesn't matter anyway, does it, Josh? *Kinner* say things without thinking them through. And of course, Nellie's suggestion was ridiculous." Her heart was hammering now, and she wasn't completely sure why.

"I didn't mean that, either..." Josh sighed heavily and took off his straw hat, running his hand through his hair. "I hope you didn't take offense is all I'm saying."

She raised her chin. "I didn't take offense." *You are lying, Lucy. But the truth is, you shouldn't have been offended. You have no desire to be close to Josh. No desire at all.*

Yet, Lucy wasn't sure that was true anymore. If it were, would she be upset at all? She was afraid to analyze her reaction too carefully. What if she didn't like what she discovered? What then?

"*Gut. Gut.* So it's all fine?" Josh asked, looking both relieved and hopeful.

"Everything is fine." She felt the stinging of tears in her eyes and blinked rapidly, willing them away.

"I'll let you get back to what you were doing then," he said and began to walk away. Only to stop and turn to her again. "What were you doing?"

"Chatting with that hen," Lucy said, pointing to the hen that was now pecking away at a little patch by the watering trough.

"Oh, you were?" he asked, mischief now twinkling in his eyes. "And what did she say back to you?"

"She was wondering whether she could have the leftovers of the casserole." Lucy smiled. Where had that silly answer come from?

He was laughing now with delight. "*Ach*, Lucy. I see why our Nellie likes you so much."

Her heart warmed at his words. Before she responded to him again, he was off, leaving her with the most wonderful feeling of having been enjoyed and, well, liked.

# Chapter Seventeen

Josh pulled into the parking lot of the Feed & Supply. He was there to buy his mother some of the special chamomile tea she liked so well. In truth, he couldn't afford the time to run this errand, but Lucy had been busy with the laundry downstairs in the basement, and he didn't mind getting away from the farm and fields for a bit.

He couldn't shake the feeling of hurt he'd seen on Lucy's face when he'd erupted out of his chair the week before during that horrid noon meal. What had he been thinking to depart so unceremoniously after his daughter's suggestion that he marry Lucy?

Was it because the thought had crossed his mind just a few days earlier? When it had, he'd been surprised to say the least. He still mourned his dear Sara. He still ached for her at the most inconvenient times. Sometimes, he thought he would go crazy with his wanting of her.

And then had come the thought to marry Lucy. He liked Lucy. He did. And she was pleasant to behold—in a way completely different from Sarah. Lucy's hair was blonde whereas Sara's had been so brown as to be nearly black. And Lucy was thinner than his Sara, more fragile looking. Although, he'd learned quickly on, Lucy was anything but fragile. With that father of hers, she'd grown tough and competent. Not someone easy to cross.

His stomach churned at the thought of Bartholomew Oyer. He had a sinking feeling he hadn't seen the last of the man, however he wished it were so. But for Lucy's sake, he hoped Bartholomew didn't return. Ever.

But he didn't appear to be a man who would give up so easily.

Josh secured the reins and jumped down from the cart, going into the Feed & Supply.

"Hello, Josh," Eliza Troyer greeted him. "How's that mother of yours doing?"

"She's improving. Thanks for asking."

"How that woman managed to avoid breaking her hip was only by the grace of *Gott*," she said, clucking her tongue. "Why, I was just talking with dear Hazel..." Eliza laughed. "You ain't interested in what I told Hazel, are you?"

Josh chuckled. "I doubt it."

"What can I help you with?"

"Just here to pick up some tea for my *mamm*."

"I've got her favorite. A new batch just came in, truth be told. I thought of her when I stocked it on the shelf."

"Thanks, Eliza. I know where it is."

"Anything else?" she asked, her expression open and warm.

"*Nee*. That will do it."

"How's your new girl working out? I've seen her with the *kinner*. They seem right fond of her."

"That they are," Josh said, horrified to realize his face was heating up. Good Lord, was he going to blush at the mere mention of Lucy's name? *Ach*, but he had to get hold of himself. He scurried from Eliza's sight to the second aisle where he knew the tea was. He was in such a hurry, he nearly knocked into two women who were scrutinizing the coffee bags.

"Goodness, Josh, you nearly bowled us over." The elder of the two was Doris Weimer. And her daughter—*single* daughter—Louise suddenly turned all smiles.

"Sorry about that," Josh muttered. "Hello Doris and Louise." He gave them both a quick nod and attempted to continue down the aisle, but Doris had other ideas.

"How is your *mamm*, Josh?"

"She's healing every day."

"So glad to hear that. Aren't you glad to hear that, Louise?" Doris elbowed her daughter.

"Right glad," Louise said, and Josh could have sworn she batted her lashes.

"We were just talking about all of you. How are the *kinner*?"

"They're fine," Josh said, itching to be gone from them.

"Louise was just thinking about bringing you some banana bread. Do you like banana bread?"

"I like it fine," Josh said.

"Is that girl still with you?" Now Doris was getting down to what she really wanted to know.

"Do you mean Lucy?" Josh asked.

"I s'pose, if that's her name."

"It is. Lucy is still with us. She's a huge help to *Mamm* as you can imagine. And the *kinner* have taken to her." Had he said too much? He didn't want to be having this conversation at all.

"I see. You know, Josh, if your *mamm* needs any other help, my Louise could come by. I mean, she's a huge help to me, but I could spare her for a while." Doris looked extremely pleased with her offer.

"That's right kind. If *Mamm* needs more help, she'll be in touch." Josh thought he'd avoided that quite nicely. And there was no way his mother would ever ask for more help. It was hard enough for her to accept Lucy's help.

"You tell her I might be by one of these days. Just to check in," Doris went on.

Josh nodded.

Doris took a step closer to him. "I hear Glenda brought over a casserole."

Josh forced himself to maintain a pleasant expression on his face. "So she did," he uttered. "You'll have to excuse me. I need to get this tea..." he reached over and grabbed a bag of chamomile tea off the shelf, "...home to *Mamm*. *Gut*-bye, ladies."

Doris looked a bit affronted to be so obviously dismissed, but Louise looked resigned. "*Gut*-bye," Doris said. She elbowed Louise, who also said, "*Gut*-bye."

Josh made his escape, paying for the tea, and getting back out to his pony cart as quickly as his legs would carry him.

It was a perfect evening. Lucy had tucked the children into bed, made sure Tamar had everything she needed, and saw that the house was straightened and ready for the next day. She was out on the porch, sitting in the porch swing. She pushed her foot gently into the floor, rocking the swing in a soft rhythmic motion. She could hear the crickets chirping and every now and again, she spotted a firefly darting about. There weren't so many anymore, not like a few weeks back. There was no wind that evening, not even a breeze. Lucy leaned against the back of the swing and closed her eyes.

*Ach,* but she liked it here. So peaceful. So still.

"Mind if I join you?"

Her eyes flew open, and she saw Josh ease himself into a nearby rocker.

"I-I don't mind," she said. "It's your porch."

He laughed. "My *mamm's* actually." He gazed out into the yard. "Beautiful evening, *ain't so?*"

"That it is." Her heart was racing with his closeness, and she prayed he wouldn't notice how nervous she'd suddenly become.

"I'm not much for just sitting, but on an evening like this… Well, it's right nice."

"After a day's work."

He looked at her then. "Are you liking it here? Are you happy?"

She blinked, not having expected to be asked such a thing. She couldn't remember a time when her happiness meant much of anything. It was an odd concept to be asked if she was happy.

"You ain't answering," he said, leaning forward. "Is something bothering you?"

"*Nee*," she said quickly. "I-I was just thinking. And *jah*. I am happy here. I like it very much."

"The *kinner* are smitten with you."

"Smitten?" She smiled at the word.

"And *Mamm* seems to have accepted you."

"We're getting along fine. It's been ... surprising."

"I don't know of anyone else who could have tamed her." He laughed heartily. "Don't you tell her I said that."

"I won't." She smiled at him.

"I'm glad you're happy here. I hope ... well, I hope you'll stay a *gut* long time."

Her heart jumped. Did that mean he wouldn't be courting soon? Did that mean he planned to resist all the women who were surely lining up?

"I'd ... I'd like that."

He nodded and then turned his gaze back to the yard. He was rocking, too, and it was as if they were rocking to the same rhythm. It was pleasant and calming. Lucy's heart settled back into its normal steady beat, but everything in her remained heightened. She glanced over at him and admired his strong profile. She imagined that under his beard, he had a strong chin. She liked the set of his nose and the way his lips turned up when he smiled. He was a handsome man, plain and simple. There was something about him that drew her.

He would never be cruel. The thought swirled through her with such an impact, her breath caught in her throat. *He would never be cruel.* He was a kind, loving man. Hadn't she witnessed first-hand over and over again how he treated his children? How he treated his mother—even when she was cantankerous?

Lucy had known that all men weren't like her father. She had known it with her head, but she hadn't known it with her heart. But now she did. Josh Lambright was a kind, loving man. And if there were other men like him in the world, then perhaps she didn't need to remain alone. Perhaps, she could marry and have children. Someday.

She smiled as she rocked. If she did ever have children, she hoped they were like Cornelia and David. Goodness, but they were precious. Oh, a handful to be sure—particularly Cornelia—but so very precious.

She continued to gaze at Josh. Her heart warmed and swelled. And then, she knew. She didn't want other men like him. She wanted ... him.

The thought lurched through her, jarring her to her core. She jumped up from the swing and it knocked her behind the legs so that she nearly toppled.

Josh noticed and was on his feet instantly. He grabbed her arm to steady her. "What is it? What's wrong?"

She felt like a fool. What was she to say? "I... I should get inside."

"But what happened? Are you all right?"

She took a huge breath. "*Jah.* I'm fine. But it's getting late, and I should be going inside."

How absurd. It wasn't late at all. The children hadn't even been in bed an hour. She could tell by the look in his eyes he knew she was lying. He knew she was making some kind of excuse.

His expression shut down. "*Gut*-night then."

She swallowed. She'd just destroyed something, and she wasn't sure what. But he was looking at her differently now. Distant. Removed.

"*G-gut* night," she said softly and skirted around him back into the house.

## Chapter Eighteen

❧

Josh watched Lucy disappear inside. What was that all about? Had he done something? As far as he could tell, they'd been sitting pleasantly enjoying a nice evening. And in truth, he'd been enjoying her company. He liked the way they could just sit and not have to say anything. It was comfortable. Peaceful.

And then she'd shot out of the swing as if stung by a bee. And she'd looked at him funny, too. Or he thought she had. Again, he yearned for Sara. There was no guessing with her. He almost always knew what she was thinking, and if he didn't, she'd tell him. She was forthright that way, and he liked it.

But Lucy? He rarely knew what she was thinking. He wished he did. He was growing more and more fond of her, despite not wanting to. He liked the way she cared for his children and his mother. And he liked the way she kept the house.

She'd stepped up beautifully when his mother became basically bedridden. She'd taken on a lot and without complaint. He liked to watch her move about the house, taking care of things.

Not that he stood there gawking at her, but he couldn't help but notice.

Was it too much? Was he expecting too much of her? But she'd told him she was happy there. Still, why had she jolted up from the swing and run into the house in such a frantic way?

And then he remembered when he'd done the same thing. Hadn't he scrammed out of the house during dinner that evening? He pressed his lips together, thinking. There had to be something bothering Lucy, and he feared it had to do with him.

*Sara, why did you have to die?* he asked into the quietness of the night.

~

It happened the next week. Josh was just coming out of the barn when a van drove in and parked under the stand of trees to the side of the yard. Just like before. Josh knew who it was even before Bartholomew crawled out of the back seat.

Josh took off his work gloves and tossed them to the ground, walking swiftly over to Bartholomew. And then he saw another man climb out of the van. Josh sucked in his breath. This couldn't be good.

"*Gut* morning," Josh said stiffly.

"Where's my daughter?" Bartholomew asked, not bothering to greet him. "Where's my Lucy?"

Josh cringed at the "my."

"Lucy's inside, I imagine," Josh said. "How can I help you?"

Bartholomew glared at him as if ready for confrontation. "This is Deacon Michael," he said brusquely. "He's here with me to fetch Lucy."

Deacon Michael gave Josh a formal nod.

"Nice to meet you, Deacon," Josh said, ensuring his voice was friendly.

Bartholomew was already walking toward the house. In two strides, Josh was up with him, the deacon following behind.

"I'll tell Lucy you're here," Josh said.

But he didn't have to tell her, for she was already at the door. Her face had gone white, and her jaw was set.

"*Dat?*"

Josh heard the tremble in her voice, and he cringed when he heard it. She was afraid even though she was trying not to show it.

"I've brought the deacon," Bartholomew said curtly.

Josh was surprised to hear that his voice had leveled out. But still, Josh had the urge to stand beside Lucy and put his arm around her waist to shore her up.

"Hello, Deacon. The *kinner* are inside," Lucy said. "We'll visit out here."

"How are you, Lucy?" the deacon asked.

"I'm fine," she answered, not looking at him. Her eyes were on her father.

"Shall we sit down," Josh suggested.

Lucy sank into a rocker, and Josh quickly sat in the one next to her, leaving the porch swing for Bartholomew and the deacon. The two of them sat. Josh thought the deacon looked uncomfortable, and he hoped it was true. Maybe he wasn't as harsh as the man he'd accompanied.

"The deacon has something to say," Bartholomew started.

"Your *dat*..." the deacon paused to take a breath, "has told me you don't want to come home."

Lucy licked her lips. "That's right."

"He's asked me to remind you that *Gott* has put fathers in authority over their daughters." The deacon glanced at Josh and then back at Lucy.

The deacon seemed to be waiting for Lucy to respond, but she sat stoically without a word.

"He is here to ask you once again to return home."

"I ain't asking," Bartholomew said. "I'm telling. It ain't necessary to ask. Lucy belongs home with me."

Josh could feel Lucy stiffen beside him. His heart went out to her, and he fought the urge to say something himself, but he knew it would only make things worse. He tried to assess just how on board the deacon was with all of this.

"We aren't trying to disrupt the peace," the deacon spoke again. "But we want to do things in order, in the way *Gott* has laid out before us."

"I understand that, Deacon," Lucy finally spoke. "I do. I also know that the family here—the Lambrights are counting on my help. The *mammi* has fallen and hurt herself, so she is unable to tend the *kinner* and the house. That is why I am here. I simply can't leave, and I feel *Gott* would not want me to."

"You can't know what *Gott* wan—" Bartholomew interrupted her, but the deacon interrupted him.

"Bartholomew, I believe we can come to a peaceful agreement here. If indeed the *mammi* has injured herself, I think Lucy could stay until she recovers. She would then come home afterward." He looked quite pleased with himself, and Josh again fought the urge to speak. He didn't want Lucy leaving after his mother was on her feet again. He wanted Lucy to stay indefinitely.

"I-I don't think so," Lucy said, but the steel had left her voice. She looked defeated, and Josh knew why. It was one thing to stand up to your father—nervy though that was. It was another thing entirely to stand up to a deacon who has been given authority over the entire community.

And by the looks on both the deacon's face and Bartholomew's face, Josh knew they were thinking the same thing.

"*Ach*, daughter, you shame me," Bartholomew sputtered, his face red. "This is the deacon. You cannot dare to defy his ruling."

The deacon had leaned forward now, toward Lucy. "You can't mean that. I have come up with a solution and—"

"But it's not a solution," Lucy cried. Then she stopped and took a heaving breath, clearly trying to calm herself. "I thank you, Deacon. Truly, I do. You have taken time to come and see me. But your solution. I... I ask that you reconsider."

"Daughter," snapped Bartholomew. "You ain't married. You haven't even been courting. You cannot turn away from—"

And then Josh did open his mouth, and he nearly choked after the words rolled from his mouth.

"That's just it," he said. "Lucy and I are to be wed."

There was instant, stunned silence—except for a crow's cry, which screeched through the air above the house. Josh was so stupefied, he could hardly breathe or think or do anything but sit there in shock. What had he just done?

Lucy was gawking at him as if he'd just grown another head. Bartholomew now gurgled, trying to get words out. The deacon's brow raised to the top of his thinning hair beneath his felt hat.

Finally, the deacon said, "That surely changes things."

Bartholomew jolted to his feet. "You're lying. You ain't engaged. You're just trying to keep your worker."

After the word "worker" came from Bartholomew's lips, Josh jumped to his feet, too.

"I'll thank you not to refer to my fiancée as my worker. She is so much more than what she does around here." He was breathing hard, and he realized he was meaning every word he said. Lucy *was* so much more than what she did. She was noble and sweet and strong and tender and kind and, well, she was wonderful.

He dared look at her now. The complete shock on her face was now overpowered by something else. Gratitude. That was what he saw. And for a fleeting moment, he knew it was all wrong. Lucy shouldn't have to feel gratitude because someone finally spoke up for her. It only compounded his suspicion that she'd never been appreciated. Oh, maybe when her mother was still alive, but not since then, and the thought made him unbalanced—both angry and sorry.

She gripped the arms of her rocker and then, she, too, was on her feet. She was staring at him, trying to read him. He saw the questions tumbling through her head. He saw her uncertainty, and he knew she was going to refute his words. She was going to deny what he had said, and he didn't want her to.

That realization was enough to make his own balance waver for a moment. But then he stepped to her, and now he did put his arm around her waist.

"We haven't set a date yet," he explained, his eyes on hers. "But that will be forthcoming soon."

She blinked and tears misted her eyes.

"Deacon, this ain't true," Bartholomew declared.

"I can hardly doubt the man," the deacon said, turning to Bartholomew. "And as they're engaged, well, Bartholomew, it looks as if you're going to have to do without your daughter."

The deacon stood and stepped forward. "Congratulations, you two."

"Thank you, Deacon," Josh said. "Can we get you some refreshment before you go?"

His words seemed to jostle Lucy out of her stupor. "Would you like some lemonade? I can also make up some sandwiches right quick."

She didn't look at Josh, but he could feel her trembling.

"*Nee*, but thank you," the deacon said. He looked at Bartholomew. "We should be going. I'm sure you'll be back for the wedding. *Gut*-bye, now. And *Gott's* blessings on you."

And with that, he headed down the steps and toward the van. Bartholomew stood shaking his head, looking lost and defeated. And angry.

He sucked in a loud breath and walked to Lucy, glaring into her eyes. "It ain't true. You've now lied to a man of *Gott*. And *Gott* won't be pleased."

And then he turned on his heel and left the porch. Lucy sagged against Josh and then as if realizing his arm was still around her, she squirmed away and sank back into the rocker. Josh waited, standing at the top of the porch steps until the van disappeared.

Only then, did he gather the courage to turn and look at Lucy. She was staring at him.

He swallowed hard and went back to the other rocker and sat down.

"What have you done?" she finally whispered.

"I... I—" he stammered.

"*Dat* was right," she said, tears now dripping down her cheeks. "It was all a lie. A lie, Josh. How could you lie to them like that?"

He shook his head. She was right, but she wasn't right. He suddenly saw the complete wisdom of marrying her. He liked her. He liked her a lot. The *kinner* liked her. His *mother* liked her. It made complete sense. He thought that were Sara alive, even Sara would like her.

*Ach, Sara, what have I done?*

"How, Josh?" Lucy asked, looking so vulnerable that he wished his arm was still around her. "How could you have done it?"

Her eyes were wide and accusing and hurt. *Ach,* he didn't want to be the one to cause her such distress.

"Because it makes sense."

"What?"

"We should marry. I ... I know it was bold of me to say so. I know you don't love me. But maybe, well, maybe you like me at least. And if we married, you wouldn't have to leave. And the *kinner*... They would have a new *mamm*." He nearly choked on those last words, feeling as if he had never betrayed anyone as he was betraying his Sara right then.

"B-but...?" Lucy's face screwed up into a huge question mark. She was having trouble digesting what he was saying.

"And *Mamm* likes you. Do you like us enough to stay, Lucy? Do you? We wouldn't have to really be married... I mean, we would be married, but we wouldn't have to..." His words dwindled off into nothing as he felt his cheeks go hot.

She stared at him, and he closed his mouth. What must she think of him?

"Are you suggesting a marriage in name only?" she asked, her voice tight and low.

"It makes sense," he said quickly. He felt an overwhelming need to convince her he was right. To sway her to agree. "It would be a *gut* life, wouldn't it? I know... Well, I gathered you didn't want to marry anyone, so wouldn't this be the perfect answer? Wedded in name only, giving you a place to live where you are deeply appreciated?"

Her expression hardened. He was saying it all wrong somehow. He blinked rapidly, trying to figure out how to phrase it properly. How to phrase it in such a way to influence her to say yes.

"And it would save you from all the single women who want to bring you food?"

He started to laugh, thinking she was being amusing, but there wasn't a hint of humor on her face. He swallowed again. "*Jah,* I guess it would."

"So we would marry to give me, the poor spinster, a place to live—a roof over my head, and a place to do my labor on this earth. And you, well, you would then be free of any potential romantic entanglements in the district. You could go about your merry way unencumbered by a real wife."

Her words cut through him. *Wait.* How did this become harsh? Or bitter? He thought he was solving both their problems. Why couldn't she see it for what it was?

She stood and squared her shoulders. He held his breath, bracing himself for what her next words might be.

"I agree," she said. His mouth dropped open, and he stared at her as she turned on her heel, pushed past him, and went into the house.

# Chapter Nineteen

Lucy could hardly walk properly as she entered the house. The minute she cleared the door, she fell back against it and stared ahead, seeing nothing.

What in the world had she just agreed to?

Marrying Josh?

He was a grieving widower who was still barely getting by. She knew that to the depth of her toes. She saw the look of pain in his eyes. She saw the way he'd sometimes tear up when he watched his *kinner*—not that he would ever admit to it, but she had seen it. She observed sometimes the slump in his shoulders and knew he was weary and thinking of Sara. Lucy wasn't sure how she knew—she just knew.

And now she was to be his wife?

*In name only. In name only. In name only.*

She mustn't forget that. He'd made his intentions quite clear. She would not be his real wife. She would only carry his name so she could stay there in Hollybrook with a roof over her head. Josh was right in that she had never intended to marry. Only recently had she begun to wonder whether she'd been hasty in that decision. Now, it didn't matter, for she *would* marry.

Only not really.

But she had agreed. Was she so very afraid of her father? Of going back home?

Or was she secretly hoping and wishing that someday she and Josh would— *Ach*, she couldn't even finish the thought. It was all so impossible and absurd. Especially now. Josh had stated what he wanted.

He wanted her as a caretaker for his children and his home, and he was willing to endure a false marriage to get both. She balked. How was this better than working for her father? Wasn't it the same thing in so many ways? Wouldn't she once again be used only for what she offered in the way of manual labor?

No. No. No.

It had to be more than that. For Josh was not cruel. Not like her father.

She thought again of how he'd spoken up with such strength to her father. She thought again of how he'd put his arm around her. She'd needed it, and she had leaned into him.

Maybe that was why the deacon had been fooled. But not her father. He'd seen it for what it was—a lie. Except wasn't Josh willing to make good on his lie?

Her mind whirled until she felt dizzy. She heard Cornelia and David begin to argue at the dining room table. She pulled herself together, took a deep breath, and went to see them.

"Lucy, David is stealin' my crayons. I wanted the blue one, and he knowed it. He took it on purpose."

"But I gotta color the sky, and the sky is blue."

"It don't have to be blue. When it's raining, it ain't blue."

"But it's blue in my picture," David insisted.

Lucy went to the table, took the blue crayon from David's hand and snapped it in two, giving one half to each of them.

"There. No need to argue now."

The two children stared up at her with surprised eyes. She let out her breath. Goodness, but she'd better get ahold of herself better than this.

"Are you mad at us?" Cornelia asked, still staring.

Lucy lowered herself to the bench. "*Nee.* I'm sorry. Breaking a crayon was a silly way to solve the problem."

David was inspecting his half. He looked up at her. "You shouldn't break crayons on purpose."

"You're right. I shouldn't have broken it. I'm sorry."

Cornelia shrugged, now clearly ready to get on with things. "Well, we each got a blue crayon now."

And they bent their heads over their work and continued. Lucy watched them in silence, realizing how much she loved them both. And now she was to be their stepmother. Their second mother. Would they be happy about it? She felt Cornelia would; she wasn't so sure about David.

Would she have children of her own someday? Her throat tightened. How could she? She was about to get married to someone who didn't really want a wife. There would be no babies for them. Would she be content with the two children sitting across from her?

She gave a soft smile then. She would concentrate on her love for these precious two little ones. Nothing else had to matter.

She heard a crunch of gravel in the drive and stood up, going quickly to the kitchen window. She peered out and saw Josh leave with the pony cart. He appeared to be in quite a hurry. Where was he going? What was so urgent? He hadn't even told he was leaving—something he usually did.

"Lucy!"

Lucy turned at the sound from the front room.

Cornelia looked over her shoulder. "*Mammi* wants you."

"So it seems," Lucy said. "I'll be back in a moment, and then maybe we can have a cookie or two. How does that sound?"

Both children gave her wide smiles. She left the room and went straight to Tamar.

"What is it? Are you needing something?"

"Was that your father? Has he come back? I was asleep so I didn't hear it all."

Lucy sat down in the rocker and pushed her foot into the floor, beginning to rock. "*Jah,* it was."

"I thought I heard more than one stranger. And then I just heard someone leaving."

"Josh had an errand to run."

Tamar studied Lucy's face, and she wanted to squirm under the scrutiny.

"So?" Tamar finally said impatiently. "What did he want this time? Your father. You to leave?"

Lucy nodded.

"Are you leaving then?"

"*Nee,*" Lucy said, not wanting to be the one to tell her what Josh had decided. "I'm staying."

"Who was the other man?"

"One of our deacons."

Tamar's eyes widened, and she sat up straighter in her makeshift bed. "Your father brought a deacon?"

Lucy nodded, feeling ashamed of both her father and herself for being the cause of such a thing.

"And you still said you wouldn't go?"

Lucy sighed. "Josh helped."

Tamar's eyes narrowed, and she studied Lucy yet again.

"What aren't you telling me?"

"I... I..." Lucy desperately tried to think of something she could say that would appease Tamar, at least for now.

"Spit it out." Tamar's expression tightened. "Might as well tell me."

Lucy sighed. "Josh told my *dat* and the deacon we were to be married."

Tamar gasped. "He did what?"

"He told them we were to be married. So now I don't have to leave. *Dat* can't make me go if I'm engaged."

"My Josh *lied* to a man of *Gott*?" Tamar asked, shaking her head, agitated. "I raised him better. His *dat* raised him better."

"But..." Lucy sucked in a huge breath. "Josh told me that we will be married. But in ... in name—" She cut off abruptly, not able to squeeze out the next word. In name *only*. But she needn't have worried. Tamar caught her meaning just the same.

Tamar clucked her tongue, fussed with the light quilt covering her, and continued to shake her head. "Josh is a fool sometimes," she said, folding her hands on top of the quilt. "A right fool."

Lucy didn't know exactly what she meant, but she feared Tamar was labeling Josh a fool because he had agreed to marry her. The thought hurt until she remembered what Tamar had said the other day at the dinner table. She looked at Tamar directly.

"What do you mean?"

"In name only. That's what you was going to say, weren't it? In name only. Goodness, but what is he thinking? Did you agree to it?"

Lucy swallowed, wishing she could disappear. "I-I did."

Tamar let out a long, protracted sigh. "I see."

Lucy bowed her head. "I s'pose you think me a fool, too."

"Look at me."

Lucy raised her head.

"I think you're falling for my son."

Now it was Lucy's turn to gasp. "*Nee*," she said quickly, shaking her head. "I'm not. I just don't want to go back home, and if Josh is willing to save me from that, well..." Her voice faded away as she listened to her vehement protest. Her cheeks went hot, and she knew she was blushing. For Tamar was right, she *was* falling for her son. She didn't want to. How she didn't want to.

She got the horrible feeling that she had just sentenced herself to a lifetime of frustration and heartache. What would it be like, married to a man she was falling in love with when she knew he had no feelings for her at all?

She closed her eyes and took a deep breath. She was going to find out.

∽

Josh leaned over the stall door and gave their milk cow a hearty slap on the shoulder. "You're looking at a fool," he told the cow. "A real fool."

He straightened up and glanced around the barn. There was plenty to be done, as always, but he wasn't in the mood for any of it. He wished he was back in Pennsylvania. He had a strong desire to go visit his wife's grave. He used to go nearly every day when they still lived close by. He'd known leaving the place and her grave would be a jolt to his system; he quite liked sitting at Sara's grave and talking about his day—imagining what she'd say in response, and how she'd look up at him with that cute half-smile of hers. He'd gone there as often as he could. Sometimes he took the children, but more often than not, he didn't. He'd leave them with the neighbor for a few minutes. Old Widow Neimer it was. She knew where he was going, so she never fussed about keeping the children.

But it wasn't easy on her, and he knew it. She was old and arthritic, but kind. Deep to the bone kind. More than once he'd been tempted to sit on her porch swing and empty his heart, but of course, he didn't. It wouldn't be fitting. So instead, he left the children and sat at Sara's feet, so to speak.

He left the barn and wandered out back to stare out over the fields.

"Can you hear me, Sara?" he asked softly. "I done a fool thing today. And then I think I made it worse. But I gave my promise, and I'll keep it. I'm to be ... married. It won't be a real marriage. Not like you and me. I just wanted to keep Lucy here. She's ... nice. And the *kinner* like her. I couldn't have their lives disrupted again. So I did the only thing I could think of. I ... well, I told her I'd marry her."

As he recounted the tale out loud, he cringed. It sounded awful. Deceitful. And he wondered again at Lucy. How must she be feeling? She'd agreed to it, but she hadn't looked happy.

She'd looked upset, troubled. Angry even. He'd insulted her somehow.

And now, as he listened to himself, he could understand it. Wasn't he basically saying he only wanted to marry her for what she could do for him? That had to be an insult. And after what he'd told her father. He'd claimed Lucy was so much more than what she did. *Ach,* and then he'd turned right around, asking her to marry him only for what she did—what she could do.

He was a horrible person.

But she'd agreed…

Besides, wasn't she marrying him only for what he could do for her? Give her a place to live away from her father. She surely didn't have any feelings for him.

He closed his eyes and raised his face to the sun and let the warmth flutter over him. Lucy wanted to be a spinster. She'd as much as told him so. She didn't have any interest in romance or love. He was sure of it.

He stood still for another minute, enjoying the heat, and then he grinned. Lucy sure did look cute when she was laughing over something Cornelia had said. And nicknaming his daughter, Nellie. Who else but Lucy would have given his daughter a nickname? Cornelia could be formidable at times, but it didn't seem to faze Lucy in the least. In truth, the two of them got on together beautifully. And little David, too. He was smitten with Lucy. More than once, Josh had seen his son cling to Lucy's hand and snuggle up against her.

Well, now neither of his children would ever have to be without Lucy. They could look on her as a mother. He gulped. He couldn't fool himself into thinking the children wouldn't soon think of Lucy as their mother. Memories of Sara would fade in time, and both of them were young. He didn't even have a photo to remind them what she looked like. He shook his head. He wished photos weren't frowned upon. He'd like to have one of Sara, himself.

But then, he would never, ever forget her or how she looked. Sara was imprinted on him so deeply that she was carved into his mind and heart.

He shuddered and headed back to the barn. Shoving his feelings aside, he got back to work.

# Chapter Twenty

It was two days since her father's visit. Josh had been gone for hours that morning, and he hadn't told anyone where he was going. Lucy wondered, but she didn't give voice to it. Tamar, however, was a different story.

"Where is that boy of mine?" she complained. "I want to take a walk, and I need him here."

Lucy turned from the front window. "I'll help you. I'm glad to. *Ach*, but it's *gut* to hear you're wanting to take a walk."

Tamar grimaced. "My hip ain't broke, though you all keep treating me like it is. I'm tired of this front room. Tonight, I'm sleeping in my own bed."

Lucy's brow rose. "Are you?"

"I can get up them stairs."

"But *Mammi, Dat* said you couldn't climb up steps," Cornelia piped up from the floor where she was playing with her doll.

"I aim to prove him wrong."

"I can help you go upstairs," Cornelia added. "Me and David are real strong."

David nodded vigorously.

"Since you're so strong," Lucy cut in, "why don't you two go transfer the chicken feed from the burlap sack into the barrel."

"Okay," Cornelia jumped up from the floor.

"Let's go," David said, running ahead of her. That, of course, only lasted a second as Cornelia raced in front of him and was out the door first.

Lucy laughed. "That girl is something, *ain't so?*"

"That she is," Tamar agreed. "You told the kids yet?"

Lucy knew immediately what she was referring to. And no, neither she nor Josh—as far as she knew—had told the children they were planning to marry. Lucy dreaded it. For saying it out loud like that—telling them—would only make it that much more real. And besides, Josh hadn't mentioned it to her again, and she half wondered whether it was still on.

And she certainly wasn't about to ask.

She bent down to pick up the doll and the wooden animals the children had scattered over the rug.

"They should do that," Tamar said.

"I know," Lucy agreed. "But I don't mind. They can clean up next time."

"You can't be spoiling them."

"I don't intend to. I'm only picking up a few toys." She heard something and stood to look out the window. "Josh is back. Looks like you'll be getting your walk, after all."

Josh pulled the pony cart up to the front porch and got out, not bothering to unhitch Crafty. Lucy heard him bound across the porch and burst into the house. He came straight into the front room.

"*Gut.* You're both here."

"Son, I'm wanting you to take m—" Tamar started, but Josh interrupted her.

"Just a minute, *Mamm.*" He looked at Lucy. "It's to be next week."

Lucy's breath caught. Did he mean…?

He turned from her to his mother. "The wedding. I've been to see the bishop. He's agreed to next week."

"Next week?" Tamar exclaimed. "We can't get everything together by next week."

"What's to get together?" he asked. "He'll come over and do it here in the front room. Of course, we'll have to move your temporary bed and push the furniture to the side, I s'pose. I reckon we can ask a few people. Not many. And Lucy..." He turned to her again. "I don't s'pose your *dat* will want to come, but you're welcome to invite him."

Lucy was frozen to the spot. Standing there, hearing Josh tick off details of their upcoming wedding as if he were inviting someone over for a cup of tea or maybe a sandwich made her stomach twist and churn. What kind of wedding was this to be? A bit of nothing with a guest or two? Something as memorable as a stale piece of toast?

It wasn't that she'd expected a full joyous wedding with all the trimmings and all the special wedding food and attendants, but she had expected more than this. It was her first and only wedding after all. And he wasn't even including her in the plans. He hadn't even done as much as ask her if the following week was all right.

My, but how kind he was, telling her she could ask her father if she wanted to.

Resentment soared through her, and she worked not to fist her hands, but to remain standing peacefully.

"Well?" he questioned. "Would he come, do you think?"

She blinked. "I-I don't know."

A silence descended then—but not a peaceful one, not a relaxed one between people who were comfortable with one another. This one stretched through the air with a thick, palpable tension that filled ever corner of the room. Josh's expression turned from determination to confusion to dread. He glanced at his mother as if looking for help.

"Son," Tamar said slowly and with deliberation, "don't you think you might ask Lucy if your plans are all right with her?"

Josh blanched and turned to Lucy. "Is this..." he gestured hesitantly with his hand, "all right with you?"

Lucy was fighting tears. She had no idea why she wanted to cry, but she did. Why should any of this matter when she hadn't been wanting to marry in the first place? When she didn't seek romance—had never sought romance of any kind? Why should she care now, all of a sudden?

This was basically a business arrangement, wasn't it?

And one she had agreed to.

"It-it's fine," she managed to stammer.

Tamar clucked her tongue as if in disgust.

Josh, still looking confused, looked from his mother to Lucy and back again. Finally, he said, "We'll tell the *kinner*. Where are they?"

"In the barn," Lucy said without feeling. "I can... I can go fetch them."

"*Nee*, I'll call them in." He moved to the door and stepped outside.

Lucy sank into a rocking chair.

"You don't have to do this," Tamar said.

Lucy drew in a deep breath. "I already agreed. Besides, it solves both our problems, *ain't so?*"

Tamar shook her head. "Fools," she muttered under her breath.

The children came running into the room.

"We only spilled a little," David told her, grinning.

"*Gut*. Thank you."

"Sit down, *kinner*," Josh said. "I was just going after you to tell you something important."

The children squeezed into a rocker together.

"Now, I have something to tell you," he started.

Lucy saw the fear on both the children's faces. David immediately stuck his fingers in his mouth. Her heart went out to them. Lately, they'd had enough bad news to be wary.

"It's all right," she said quickly, putting on a smile. "Nothing is wrong."

*Yes, it is. Yes, it is. Yes, it is.*

"Lucy and I..." Josh took a breath. "Lucy and I are to be married."

Cornelia's face screwed up and then she jumped out of the rocker. "So, she ain't leaving?"

Josh smiled. "*Nee*, she ain't leaving."

"*Gut!*" Cornelia grabbed David's hand. "Let's go back to the barn. I wanna feed the chickens with that new seed."

And the two of them tore out of the house. Lucy blinked in their wake. That was it? That was their whole reaction? She shook her head and couldn't help but start to laugh. Here she was, acting as if the world was slipping from its axis, and there the children were—taking it in stride as if nothing out of the ordinary was happening at all.

Josh stood there watching her, looking completely baffled. As Lucy watched him, she started laughing harder, and then she realized her laughter was about to turn into tears and she rushed from the room, climbing the stairs, and throwing herself on her bed, where the tears did indeed, come.

Josh looked at his mother. "What ... what was that?"

Tamar shook her head. "That was an upset woman."

"She was laughing."

"To keep from crying."

Josh sighed audibly. "What are you talking about?"

"I reckon she's up there crying right now."

Josh's eyes narrowed. "Since when did you start taking Lucy's side in anything. You don't even like her."

"I never said I didn't like her. I didn't want her here. It ain't the same thing."

"Well, now you appear to be on her side."

"When did this become about sides?"

Josh sank onto the couch by his mother's feet. "I don't know. I just... She did seem upset, didn't she?"

Tamar only looked at him.

"Maybe she don't want to get married after all."

"She doesn't want to go back home."

"I know," he cried. "That's why I suggested it in the first place."

His mother shook her head again, her lips pursed in that awful disapproving pout he saw so often.

"What?" he asked sharply. "What?"

"It just seems mighty cold is all. This whole thing."

His jaw tightened. "What would you have me do? The *kinner* like her. I don't want her to leave."

His mother smoothed the quilt over her lap. She fussed with the seams as if inspecting it at a state fair for a prize. Then she looked up at him.

"You sure that's the only reason?"

He gaped at her. "What other reason could there be?"

"You like her."

He scowled impatiently. "Of course, I like her. I wouldn't want her watching my *kinner* otherwise."

Tamar leaned forward and rested her hand on his thigh. "You know what I mean."

He flicked her hand from his leg and then realized how abrupt he was being. He grabbed up her hand again and held onto it.

Tamar shook her head. "There ain't nothing wrong if you do."

"I know that."

"Do you?" she questioned. "Do you truly know that?"

He released her hand and stood up. "I have chores to do. I've already wasted most of the morning being gone."

"Wasted?" Tamar questioned, raising her brow.

He groaned. What was wrong with his mother that day? She was downright pushy and annoying. And since when did she care so much about Lucy anyway? He'd known they were getting along much better, but still. Couldn't his mother understand things from his point of view? Couldn't she see this was a simple arrangement? One both he and Lucy had planned and agreed to?

He left the house and strode quickly across the yard. Both he *and* Lucy had planned? Lucy hadn't planned one bit of anything. He'd done it all. But he was trying to hurry things up. Get everything done so it couldn't be undone.

He'd been telling the truth. He didn't want Lucy to leave and to return to her father. Any kind-hearted man would feel the same way about it. Lucy's father was a heartless man, and he treated Lucy badly.

Josh didn't want that for Lucy.

She deserved so much more…

*Like a husband in name only?*

He stopped abruptly and moaned. He turned slowly on his heel and stared up at Lucy's bedroom window. Was his mother right? Was she up there crying? Had he bungled things when all he'd wanted to do was make arrangements?

His breathing went shallow, and he felt regret. Had he hurt Lucy when he'd been trying to save her from hurt? No. Surely not. Surely, she understood what he was doing and why. Surely, she was grateful everything was falling into place—and quick-like.

He thought he saw her curtain swish to the side. He blinked and focused more intently but saw nothing further. No movement. No shadow. He shrugged, sighed again, and turned to head back to the barn.

The chores wouldn't be doing themselves, now, would they?

⁓

Lucy stepped back, afraid she'd been seen. Why had Josh been staring up at her window, anyway? Goodness, but she hoped he hadn't seen her. She hadn't been spying on him; in fact, she was surprised when she saw him walk so quickly toward the barn. She figured he'd still be with Tamar discussing the upcoming wedding.

*Ach*, but what had she gotten herself into? Did she truly want to marry the man? And what would happen if…?

She let the question dangle in her mind. She was treading into dangerous territory, and she knew it. She wasn't completely insensitive to things of the heart. And she feared—no, she knew—she was beginning to have real feelings for Josh. When she'd first come, she'd been so careful. She'd stayed clear of him as much as she could. But that had proven impossible. And then she'd explained her growing feelings for him as compassion and even pity. He was struggling with his grief. She could see it even if he tried to hide it. But now? Standing here at the window crying as if her heart were breaking?

That could hardly be explained as compassion or pity.

Except maybe for herself. She was growing fond of Josh, more than fond, truth be told. But in his eyes, she was a convenience. She was someone to take care of his children and his mother. She was someone to clean his house and cook his meals.

As she had thought before, she might as well be back at her father's house.

She grabbed the edge of the curtain. No. She was being overly dramatic. This wasn't the same as her father's house at all. She didn't have to walk about fearing his lashing tongue. She didn't have to wonder when he might strike her again in his anger. She didn't have to dread getting up every morning.

She licked her lips and sniffed. Maybe in time, Josh would become fond of her. That one time—when they'd spoken in the barn—he'd acted almost tender with her. Maybe there was hope for a future beyond what he predicted. Maybe there was hope he'd grow to love her.

But did she really want to put herself through that?

She let go of the curtain and smoothed down the wrinkles she'd made. She wiped the tears from her eyes and walked to the door of her bedroom. One thing was sure—she couldn't hide up here all day. There were chores to be done. Children to be looked after. And a temperamental *mammi* to watch over.

## Chapter Twenty-One

Bartholomew didn't feel well. His shoulders hurt, and the back of his neck hurt, too. Sometimes the pain spread up into his head. He wasn't one who got headaches, generally, but ever since that disastrous trip to Hollybrook, things had changed.

For the worse. For the much, much worse.

He'd thought taking Deacon Michael with him was a brilliant idea. How could Lucy deny a deacon? He held even more authority than a father did. But the deacon had been worthless to him. Worse than worthless. The man had even blessed Lucy for staying.

And marrying.

What kind of farce was that? For Bartholomew was certain Lucy had known nothing about the marriage before Josh had mentioned it. That Josh Lambright was a slick fellow. A liar, in fact. For Bartholomew had seen the look of shock on his daughter's face. There was no way the two of them were engaged.

He'd wanted to press the point, wanted to force the truth out of the two of them. But no. He'd brought that useless deacon, so he had to mind his manners. But that didn't mean it was over. No, it was far from over, as far as Bartholomew was concerned. He simply needed another plan. Another way to get Lucy home.

Lord, but his head was hurting. He had no desire to go outside and see to the crops. He had no desire to do anything but sit there and seethe. And so he did.

It didn't take long to come up with another plan. And it was brilliant. He didn't feel well. He *wasn't* well. Lucy was needed to take care of him. She could hardly turn away if he needed her because of illness. Despite her recent coldness to him, he knew her well. She would not turn away in his hour of need.

And that Josh fellow could well and good get someone else to take care of his children and his mother.

Grinning now, and his headache easing, he stood up to get his tablet and pen. He'd dash off a letter right quick. If he could catch the mailman in time, the letter would get to Lucy the next day—or the day after at the very latest.

"You're coming home, daughter," he mumbled with satisfaction. "And once you're here, you ain't leaving again. I'll make sure of that."

He didn't bother to figure out those last details. It was enough that he'd get her to come home. And he'd be nicer this time. He wasn't a total idiot. He knew he hadn't been the nicest person since his Janet died. He could change that. Not that he had plans to coddle the girl, far from it. She needed to understand life was hard.

But maybe, he could soften himself a bit. He would start looking around for someone to court her, too. She wasn't a bad-looking sort, and there was room in his old farmhouse for Lucy's husband and any children that might come along.

He sat down at the dining table and set the tablet before him. He got busy writing, making sure to sound ill and needy. *Ach,* but it felt good to be doing something again. His plan would work. He knew it would.

∽

Lucy stared at the envelope with dread. In truth, she'd been expecting to hear from her father again. She knew he was furious when he'd left with the deacon. And she feared he hadn't taken her engagement seriously.

She scooted the envelope around on the table, trying to decide whether she should open it or not. If she didn't, though, she could be surprised with another visit. But then, was she in the mood for a huge scolding? For she was certain that was what the letter contained.

She had to know. Staring at the thing did nothing but upset her.

With a huge sigh, she picked up the envelope and ripped it open, spreading the letter out on the table before her. Her eyes widened as she read.

*Dear Lucy,*

*I'm sorry for the way we ended our visit of the other day. You know all I want is for you to come home. You belong here in your hometown where you grew up. Where your* mamm *and I raised you.*

*I am not well, Lucy. I have pain in my shoulders and neck and head. I have tried to find relief, but I can't. At times, I'm unable to do the simplest of tasks. I need your help.*

*I would understand if you can't come to help me. I know you are caring for that whole family in Hollybrook. But if you could find your way to come for at least a couple of days, it would be a great blessing to me.*

*I must stop writing now. Even this is taxing my strength.*

*Your father*

. . .

Lucy scooted back from the table, staring at the letter as if it were alive. Her father, ill? Was this a trick? The minute she thought it, she felt guilty. Her father wouldn't out and out lie to her like that, would he? Was he really sick?

And there was no one to help him. He wasn't on good terms with their only kin in town—except for Greta. And considering that Greta had helped Lucy find this job, she imagined her cousin had fallen from his esteem, too. If he'd found out the truth of it, anyway. And her father hadn't taken her suggestion to get someone in during the day. He was waiting for her to come home.

So, he was all alone.

She took in a long breath and read the letter again. He sounded almost ... nice. And if she didn't come, he said he would understand. Fine, then. She wouldn't go. She wasn't under any obligation to go, was she?

Shame burned through her. He was her father. He'd reached out for help. Of course, she was under obligation.

But what of her wedding? She couldn't get that put together and be gone at the same time. Well, it would just have to be pushed back. Josh would understand. She winced. Why would he care anyway? As long as she promised to return, as long as they remained engaged, he should be happy enough. But she needed to tell him.

She stuck the letter back into its envelope and tucked it beneath her waistband. Then she went outside to find him. He was out in the fields, but not far. She stood at the edge of the crop and waved. He saw her almost instantly and came traipsing through the rows until he stood in front of her.

"Lucy? Something wrong?"

"I need to go back home," she blurted.

His brow creased. "What? Why? Is your *dat* here?"

She took a breath. "*Nee,* he ain't. But he's written, and—"

"And you're leaving?" he cut in. "But with the engagement, you don't have to go. You're not obligated."

"It ain't that," she said, pulling the envelope from her waistband. "Here."

Why didn't she just tell him herself? Why hand him the letter? She had no idea, but she sometimes felt befuddled in Josh's presence, which was distressing and annoying.

He read through the letter quickly. "Sick, huh?"

"*Jah.* And it's true, he has no one to help him. Our only family there... Well, except for my cousin, they don't get along well."

"Then your cousin can help."

"He wouldn't ask her. And I think he's likely mad at her."

"He can hire someone."

Josh's voice was curt and harsh, and Lucy felt a desire to defend her father rush up within her.

"He's unwell, Josh. He needs me. I don't need to stay long. In fact, I can go and arrange for someone to help him so I can return here."

"And you will plan to return?"

His impatient tone startled her. "Of course, I do. I've made a promise, haven't I?"

But at that very moment, she wished she could take the promise back. And he was standing too near her, much too near. She squirmed under his close scrutiny and felt the desire to run. But she didn't. She raised her chin slightly to give herself courage. Yet the very fact that she needed courage was troubling.

She had no reason to be afraid of Josh. He had never hurt her, nor would he. She was clear on that.

*Are you clear?* The voice in her head blared. *People get hurt in all sorts of ways.*

She blinked. "I'll be back soon."

"What about our wedding next week?" he asked.

"We'll have to change the date."

He stared at her, and she began to squirm all over again. "To when?" he asked, but this time his voice was subdued.

"I-I don't know. Can't we decide when I return?"

"And what about the *kinner* in the meantime? What about *Mamm*?"

But he didn't say, *What about me?* And the omission was like a piercing arrow. Her heart twisted and plunged to her feet. *Won't you miss me, too?*

Thoroughly annoyed with the way her mind was playing with her, she went on. "I'm sure one of the many single women in the district will be glad to come in for a bit."

It was true, and the thought rankled. But Josh did need someone. Tamar was on her feet more these days, but she could hardly watch the children and do the cooking and cleaning as well.

"Is that what you want?" Josh asked, and then his face went red. "I-I'm sorry. If you feel you should go, then you go. I... *Jah*, I will ask Eliza, and she'll find me someone."

Lucy swallowed; her throat was dry, and it scratched all the way down. "All right," she murmured.

"So you think it's true?" he asked, handing her the letter back.

Her breath caught. "He wouldn't lie to me."

He nodded slowly, and she could see he wasn't convinced. She had a sudden wish that he and the family would come with her, but that was an absurd thought. He had a farm to look after, crops to grow, and animals to tend. But most of all, he wouldn't want to come, so there was no hope in even thinking about it.

"Will you leave tomorrow?"

"*Jah*." Their gazes held then, and she felt as though her entire being rose up to meet him. She held her breath, hardly realizing it. She was filled with wanting. And waiting.

But waiting for what? A gesture? A touch?

And then he did touch her. His hand grazed her arm and settled for a brief moment on her shoulder before dropping away. Something intense flared through her, and there was a tingling in the pit of her stomach and a burning on her shoulder. Did he feel it too? This connection or whatever it was between them? It was as real to her as the air she breathed.

She leaned toward him ever-so-slightly, hardly knowing she did so. And then his eyes left hers, and awkwardly, he cleared his throat.

"Well, you, uh, better get packing. I'll tell the *kinner*."

"*Nee*," she said quickly. "I'll tell them. And your *mamm*."

"Cornelia won't understand. Or she'll choose not to."

Lucy shook her head and slipped back into employee mode. "She'll be fine. I'll explain everything."

"You'll ... say *gut*—" He stopped abruptly and though he still only stood inches in front of her, she could feel a growing distance between them. "Never mind."

She frowned, not liking this coldness from him. It was exactly the same as it had been when she'd first arrived, a calculated distance, a hesitancy, a formality.

"I'll buy my ticket from the bus driver tomorrow."

Josh nodded and turned around to make his way back into the fields.

~

"You can't go!" Cornelia cried. "*Dat* said you was gonna be married."

"We are," Lucy said for the third time. "But my *dat* is sick, and I must go and take care of him for a while."

"Then me and David are going, too."

Lucy sighed. "I wish I could take you, but I can't. Goodness, but your *dat* would miss you something terrible. And your *mammi*, too. Besides, who's going to help take care of everything while I'm gone."

David had been noticeably quiet through the whole interchange, but now he spoke up. "You ain't coming back."

"But I am," Lucy insisted.

David set his jaw and shook his head. "You ain't coming back."

"Remember how you were worried *Mammi* wouldn't come back? Remember? After her accident? I told you she'd come back, and she did. This is the same thing. I'm leaving for a little while, and then I'll come back."

David chewed on his lower lip and some of the tension visibly left his body. "How are you going to swing me?"

Lucy laughed. "Well, I can't swing you from my home, but when I get back, I'll swing you for double the usual time. How would you like that?"

David grinned. "I like that."

"*Gut*. Then we have an agreement, all right?"

He nodded.

"How about swinging me?" Cornelia asked.

"*Ach*, Nellie," Lucy said, grabbing her up in her arms. "Whatever am I going to do without you? I'll miss you like a mama deer misses her fawn."

"What's a fawn?" David asked.

"I'm not a deer," Cornelia said.

"A fawn is a *boppli* deer, and of course, you're not a deer, Nellie."

Cornelia appeared somewhat mollified. "When are you leaving?"

"Tomorrow."

David scowled. "That's soon."

"*Jah*, it is," Lucy said. "But the sooner I go, the sooner I can come back."

"I thought you didn't like your *dat*," Cornelia announced.

Lucy sucked in her breath. What had the child overheard? "He's my *dat*, so ... of course, I should like him."

Lucy was talking in riddles to keep from lying, but who was she fooling? If even Cornelia had put that together, Lucy's efforts to deny it would likely go unbelieved—which was quickly proved.

Cornelia shook her head. "*Nee*. You don't. And *Dat* don't like him neither. So, you shouldn't have to go at all." She crossed her arms over her chest and gave a determined nod.

Lucy gave the girl a squeeze. "He is my *dat,* and I am going. Now, who wants to help me pack?"

Cornelia and David nodded and raced directly up the stairs to Lucy's room. Lucy followed much more slowly, her dread of going home growing stronger with each step.

## Chapter Twenty-Two

Lucy didn't want Josh to take her to the bus station, but he wouldn't hear of anything else. And as it turned out, Cornelia and David went along for the ride, and the two of them kept the chatter going the entire way there. Lucy was so grateful for this, she could have hugged and kissed them both—which she did when they said good-bye.

Josh got out with her, though he told the children to stay put. He pulled out her bag.

"Did you pack up all your things?"

She nodded. She hadn't come with all that much in the first place, so it only made sense to pack it all up. Depending on how long she stayed, she might need all her clothes.

Josh took her bag to where two other passengers were waiting. He turned to her. "So this is it."

"For now," she added quickly. "I'll see you soon."

"You going to write?"

"Do you want me to?" Of course, Lucy had already planned on writing—to the children and Tamar at least. But indirectly, her letters would be to Josh, too, for he would surely read them when they were delivered.

He shrugged. "Suit yourself."

She inhaled, pretending his comment didn't hurt her feelings. "I'll write to the *kinner* ... and your *mamm*."

The sudden flame she saw in his eyes startled her, but it was gone so quickly, she wasn't sure if it had been there at all. She reached down and picked up her bag, moving it closer to her feet.

"*Gut*-bye, then," she said crisply.

He nodded and touched the brim of his straw hat. Then he turned and left her. He got into the buggy and for a moment, she heard David say something, but she couldn't make it out from where she stood. Then the buggy was moving, going back to the house and the farm. Only this time, without her inside.

Bartholomew was bound and determined Lucy's visit was going to go well. So well, in fact, that she would decide to stay home. He'd been beyond relieved when word came that she'd left a message in the phone shanty saying she was arriving that day. He'd made sure her room was tidy and that there was a fresh towel and washrag in the bathroom for her. But he purposely left the kitchen in a mess, not that he would have cleaned it anyway. And the house needed sweeping and the laundry needed done.

He stood back and surveyed the messiness of it all. Perfect. Lucy would see clearly how much she was needed.

And he was going to be nice. She wanted nice—he would give it to her.

He reached back and tried to rub out some of the kinks in his neck, but it was useless. He had that headache again, too, although it had lessened because Lucy was coming home. He was sure that was why.

For a moment, his anger got the better of him again. She should have never left. He should have never let her go. Stupid move. One he wouldn't make again.

He tried to relax his jaw. When he clenched it, his headache got worse. He took a slow, deliberate breath.

*Nice. Remember, be nice.*

He walked out to the porch and sat in the swing, which creaked under his weight. He was hungry, but he wasn't going to start fussing about trying to find something to eat. Lucy would be home soon enough.

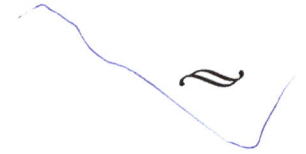

~

Lucy sat stiffly on the bus. She tried to relax, but it was fruitless. And she tried to stop thinking, but her mind was running in circles. All her life she'd been taught family was everything. Being loyal was everything. Being faithful was everything.

She'd lived her life on those principles—except when she'd left home without her father's blessing.

And now, here she was, returning. How had this happened? Why had she dropped everything to run to his aid so quickly? She had left for a reason—a *good* reason. But now, here she was going back. She should have taken more time to investigate things.

Josh thought her father might be lying. That had chafed—even though the suspicion had flown through her mind, too. But somehow, hearing it from someone else's lips had caused her loyalty to surge.

Still, she could have communicated with her father, and not just run back to him. She could have written him, asked more about his illness. She could have even written Greta and asked for her opinion. But Lucy had a feeling Greta wouldn't know for it wasn't like her dad to announce such things.

Considering illness a weakness, he would simply demand his own daughter to help.

But that was the thing. He hadn't demanded. He'd asked. His tone had been surprising, to say the least. Maybe he'd turned over a new leaf. Maybe, he'd become kinder and more compassionate during these days alone.

She had to admit she hoped so. She yearned to have her father back—the father she remembered when her mother had been alive. They had gotten on well during those days. In truth, she didn't have a lot to do with him as he stayed busy in the fields. He had cursed his luck with only having one child—and that one a daughter. Yet Lucy's mother had always softened that blow, and everything had righted itself.

Lucy wondered now how often her mother had run interference. How often had she buffered her father? Maybe he had never been the nice father she remembered.

But now? She glanced down at her purse where her father's letter was tucked away. Now could be their chance at a new beginning. She could care for him until the worst had passed, and then she could make arrangements for someone to take over when she left. And perhaps her father would come to her wedding.

She swallowed. The thought of her wedding gave her no joy at all. She would have thought marrying the man she was growing to love would be a pleasant thought—even if he didn't love her back, for she would still be with him; she would still be sharing his life.

But the thought left her mouth filled with dust. What woman wanted to be yoked to a man who didn't love her?

She closed her eyes and sighed. She was doing it to get away from her father. But if her father had changed—if he would treat her with respect—then maybe she didn't have to get away from him at all. She wouldn't have to marry Josh.

She pressed her hand against her heart and took a deep breath. If she didn't go back, she wouldn't ever see Josh again. Nor precious little Nellie and David. Nor Tamar. Could she live with not ever seeing them again?

She didn't want to. They were so dear to her.

And she had promised to return.

But truthfully, would Josh really care? It wouldn't take him long to find someone else to watch the children and mind the house. It didn't really matter, did it, if it was her? All he really needed was an able-bodied woman.

She opened her eyes and forced herself to watch the speeding scenery go by. She needed to stop thinking. She was making herself miserable with her morose thoughts. Goodness, but she wished little Nellie was beside her chattering away.

The thought made her smile, and she spent the rest of the bus ride thinking of the children and the silly things they did and said.

When the bus pulled to a huffing stop, her gloomy thoughts descended once again. She tried to push them aside, but a sense of foreboding had taken over, and she couldn't seem to shake it. She gathered up her belongings and scooted her way down the narrow aisle and out the door. She took her suitcase from the driver who was unloading a few other pieces of luggage from the underside of the bus.

She glanced around, hoping her father had gotten her phone message and would be there waiting for her. At first, she didn't see him, but then behind a buggy, she spotted their pony cart. Her father was sitting on the driver's bench, hunched.

"*Dat*," she called and skirted around the buggy to face him.

"You're here," he said. He gave her a smile, but something about it bothered her. But then, he was likely in pain. People who didn't feel well, didn't give genuine smiles, did they?

She put her luggage in the back of the cart and climbed up to sit by her father. The bench was small, and she had to press up against him to fit. She didn't much like it, but there was no apple crate in the back, which she usually used as a seat.

"How are you feeling?" she asked.

He gave a grunt and then flashed her the same forced smile. "I'm making do."

"Well, I'm here now," she said. "I can help."

He nodded and snapped the reins. The cart jolted into motion, heading toward home. Lucy felt decidedly uncomfortable. She tried to think of something to say, but her mind was filled with the Lambrights, and she knew her father wouldn't want to hear about them.

"Um... How are the crops doing?" she finally ventured.

He glanced sideways at her and then back to the road. "Now you're home, they'll get better. I haven't spent much time out there."

"I see."

"I'm hungry. You can get a meal ready when..." He paused for a moment, and then said slowly, as if carefully choosing his words, "Are you hungry?"

She blinked in surprise. Was he really concerned for her? This was indeed new. A wave of hope rushed through her. "I am hungry. I'll fix us both a hearty noon meal."

"Sounds *gut*," he said.

They fell into silence again, Lucy ruminating on the changes in her father. He seemed different, for sure and for certain. Even the way he sat appeared different. He appeared smaller somehow, shrunken. He must truly not be feeling well.

"Do you need to rest when we get home?" she asked.

He shook his head. "*Nee.*"

"What did the doctor say? You did go see one, didn't you?"

He didn't answer at first, and she felt her hopes dampen. He'd never been a proponent of *Englisch* medicine and doctors, but he wasn't really against them either. He'd gone on occasion, and so had she. And if he was so ill that he needed her, he should have gone.

"*Dat*, you didn't go?"

"Why should I when you were coming home?" he said crossly. Then he swallowed, and his voice softened. "I mean, I'll go later if I need to."

She frowned. "I'm sorry. I shouldn't be asking you all this. I know you're not feeling well, and I appreciate you coming to fetch me. You could have sent Glenda..."

He shook his head. "*Nee.* I wanted to fetch you myself." At this, he gave her another smile, though this one seemed more genuine. "I'm right glad you're back."

"I can't stay too long, though," she said, feeling as if she needed to prepare him. "Josh and I are to be married quite soon."

Something flickered in his eyes, and she braced herself. But his voice was even when he said, "Thank you for telling me."

Lucy felt more unsettled with this new version of her father than with the older version. At least before, she knew what to expect. This newer version seemed to be all over the place. She straightened her back. No matter. She was here to help him, and that was what she was going to do.

# Chapter Twenty-Three

Josh threw up his hands in frustration. "Cornelia, I've told a hundred times not to bother your brother."

"My name is Nellie," Cornelia insisted, her lip protruding in a pout.

"She hitted me," David said, rubbing his arm.

"And hitting is completely unacceptable," Josh continued. "You know that. Violence never solves anything."

"I wasn't being violent," Cornelia countered. "I just hit him a little, tiny bit."

Josh took a deep breath. "Hitting a little, tiny bit is still hitting. Now both of you go to your rooms for a while. I'll call you down later."

The two children glowered at each other and then clomped up the stairs. Josh shook his head and was about to go back outside when his mother called him.

He went to the front room. "*Jah, Mamm?*"

"Get her back."

"Huh?"

"You know what I mean. Get Lucy back."

"Her *dat* is sick."

"I know that, but I don't trust that man. Get her back. Who knows what might happen while she's there?"

Josh sighed. He'd like nothing more than to get Lucy back. "She wanted to go, *Mamm*. What could I have done?"

"Did you tell her you'd miss her? Did you tell her things won't be the same around here until she returns?"

He stared at her.

She clicked her tongue and shook her head. "You didn't, did you? Did you tell her you love her?"

Josh balked. "What? What are you talking about? This isn't a love match. You *know* that."

"There are many things I know, son. And one of them is you're falling for her. I don't blame you. The girl won me over." Tamar chuckled. "Not completely, though, so don't go getting confused."

Josh was so surprised, he couldn't say a word. His mother hadn't spoken this much about anything for a long time. In truth, she didn't talk with him much beyond the basic necessities. He thought again about how Lucy had made inroads with his mother. He thought again about how Lucy wheedled her way into everyone's heart.

But *his* heart?

His mother didn't know everything. And besides—

"Son?" Tamar interrupted his thoughts. "Go get her back."

"What am I supposed to do?" he asked. "Just show up and force her back here? Like her father tried to do?"

Tamar was silent then. She sighed. "*Nee.* I s'pose you're right on that."

"I need to get back to work," he said. "Do you need anything before I go back out?"

Tamar shook her head. "The *kinner* upstairs?"

"*Jah*. They've been sent to their rooms for a bit. I reckon they can come back down shortly."

Before he left the house, he heard Cornelia and David upstairs, laughing gleefully together, enjoying some game or the other. He chuckled under his breath. They never stayed at odds for long. They liked each other too much.

∼

Lucy set to putting the kitchen to rights immediately. Some of the dishes must have been used days ago for she almost needed a chisel to get the food grime to come loose. But after a full hour of hard work, it was back to its normal state. She searched through the cupboards, taking inventory of what food she could find. Had her father even gone once to the mercantile since she'd left? It certainly didn't appear that way, but then, he'd been sick so that would account for it.

She began to make a list of what was needed. That afternoon, she could hitch the pony cart back up and take it to the store. The weather was beautiful—the sun shining brightly in the bluest of skies. There was a light breeze, too, evidenced by the swaying branches of the willow in the front yard.

But first, she had to fashion together some kind of noon meal for the two of them. There was a frozen roast, but there was no time for it to thaw. She did put it in the refrigerator, though. It could be baked the following day. She finally settled for egg salad sandwiches. She had found a half loaf of bread; although, it was a bit stale.

"*Dat?*" she called toward the front room. "Dinner is on the table."

Her father appeared quickly. "I'm right hungry."

"It's only sandwiches for today. I'll go into town later and get some more supplies. Tomorrow, I'll have something hot for you."

He grinned appreciatively. "That sounds *gut*."

She half-expected him to complain and was pleasantly surprised when he didn't. This also gave her hope that he had indeed changed. He led them in a silent blessing and then began to eat.

"Do you need to rest this afternoon? Should I see to the animals?"

He blinked as if confused, and then said, "*Jah*, that is a *gut* idea. Maybe if I rest a bit, I'll be able to do more tomorrow."

"I hope so. I still think it would be best to see a doctor."

He put down his sandwich and shook his head. "I already feel better just having you here."

His heartfelt words were such a shock, she had no idea how to respond. But her heart warmed to them, and she was glad she had come home. To see her father like this, to hear his words, were a healing balm, and she had a sudden urge to sit with him all afternoon and simply be together. But there were chores to be done, and she had never shirked her responsibilities before. There would be plenty of time later to be with her father.

Indeed, that evening after she finished with the supper dishes, they would have time to sit together. Maybe they could go out onto the porch. It was always pleasant this time of year. She shook her head, remembering how rigidly she'd avoided being with him if she could. She went to any lengths to avoid sitting with him, but now, all she wanted to do was be with him.

*Ach*, if she'd known that leaving him would cause such a change, she would have left years ago, only to come back home to a new father.

~

Bartholomew felt a deep satisfaction in his soul. He sat lazily on the davenport, ready to drift off to sleep. His plan was working and working beautifully. Lucy was home. And if he wasn't mistaken, she was fairly happy to be there. He was doing his utmost to be pleasant and agreeable, and it was working. He grinned. There was no way she'd want to return to Hollybrook when he was finished.

She wouldn't want to leave him to fend for himself. She'd be eager to stay on and manage the house and the meals.

Good. Because he was sorely sick of fending for himself. And he didn't want to admit to his sister and her family that Lucy had left without his blessing. And his niece, Greta. He had loved her since her birth and had always felt particularly close to the girl. But he knew the truth of it now. Greta had helped

# THE RECENT WIDOWER

Lucy find that miserable job in Hollybrook, and he was never going to forgive her for it. Never. How dare she betray him like that?

And Lucy's suggestion to find someone to come in was also out of the question. He didn't want strangers in his house. He wanted Lucy. She was his daughter, and this was where she belonged.

His smile widened with the thought. He'd done well getting her to come home. So what if he'd had to exaggerate a little. He was feeling poorly—just not as poorly as Lucy thought. But he could play the part for a day or two. By then, Lucy would be back in the routine of things, and all would be well.

∼

As Lucy went mechanically about her tasks of cleaning up the house, her mind had plenty of time to wander. She was missing the children and even Tamar's caustic comments. But most of all, she was missing Josh. She was quite certain he wasn't missing her. Oh, he would be missing the work she did for him, there was no question about that. But he wouldn't be missing her, and the thought stung.

On her fourth day home, her father had felt good enough to wander out to the fields to do some work. He moved slowly, which she was growing accustomed to, but he did go outside. She was relieved as she was finding it difficult to keep up with the house and the meals and the animals and all the other outside chores.

Now, she was dusting. She went into her father's bedroom. She never liked coming in here, for the memories of her mother and their happy times sitting together on the big bed remained sharp and painful. But it was well beyond time to stop suffering over such things, and Lucy walked more boldly inside this time. She purposefully looked at her mother's pale blue dress that hung on the peg behind the door.

Her father had refused to take it down and put it away. Years before, that dress had haunted Lucy, the way it hung, empty and lifeless. It had been her mother's favorite, the dress she wore to all special occasions. She'd looked beautiful in it, too, like what Lucy imagined a fairy princess looked like. She never said so, though, for fear of being scolded. Amish children didn't talk about fairy princesses.

But Lucy had read a book once in the public library. Well, she hadn't read it cover to cover, for she hadn't had the time. She was poring over it on the floor beside a long bookshelf, flat on her stomach, her legs stretched out behind her, when her mother had come and told her it was time to go back home. Lucy wasn't allowed to check the book out, so she left it there, open on the floor, its bright pages brilliant with colorful images of fairies and princesses fluttering enticingly.

Lucy had never forgotten those images, and she especially remembered them when her mother put on her blue dress.

Lucy had been almost sure than when her mother turned around, there would be fairy wings on her back, flapping softly.

Now, Lucy stood completely still and stared at the blue dress. After an initial pang, she didn't feel anything. She stood there a moment longer, waiting for the certain pain and yearning that would follow, but all she felt was a soft remembrance, a gentle reminder of the wonderful mother she'd had. Tears flooded her eyes as she realized she was finally getting over it.

But why? It had been five years since her mother had passed, and it had never left her. What had changed? Josh's image flashed through her mind, and then the children's faces, and then Tamar's. Did they have something to do with it? She couldn't imagine how.

She began by dusting the top of her father's dresser and then the tops of his nightstand. She took a moment to straighten some papers on the nightstand shelf, what appeared to be miscellaneous mail. As she straightened up to move to his bed frame, one envelope slipped from the pile. She bent to retrieve it from the floor and stopped cold.

The envelope was addressed to her. How could that be? She hadn't gotten mail for years. Was this some old piece of correspondence she'd long forgotten about. But then she glimpsed the return address ... *Hollybrook*.

He heart leapt to her throat, and she tore the envelope open. Three pieces of paper fluttered to the bed. She grabbed them up. The first was a drawing of a rainbow and a bird. That surely was from Cornelia. The next were some scribbles and a stick figure of a dog, or what could be a dog. David. And the third... Her gaze flew to the end, and she saw Josh's name. Her breath caught.

*Dear Lucy,*

*I suppose it's quite soon to be writing, but the* kinner *were bent on sending you their drawings. Cornelia said to tell you to hurry up and come back.*

Mamm *is getting along, but I know she misses you, too.*

*I hope your* dat *is feeling better. In truth, I hope he's well again. When do you plan to come back?*

*Josh*

Lucy read it again, trying to discern Josh's mood when he wrote it. She couldn't help but notice he hadn't said he missed her. But then, why would he say it? He didn't miss her; she was certain of that. But he did ask when she was returning. That was something, wasn't it?

But what was disturbing was why had her father not given her the letter? And when had he gone out to the mailbox to get it? The last couple days, he'd been too weak to do much of anything. She'd fetched the mail; although now that she thought about it, there hadn't been any mail at all the last two days.

Had he planned to sneak out there in case Josh had written?

She frowned and bit the corner of her lip. He wouldn't do that, would he? Not the way he was now. Before, she wouldn't have been surprised in the least. But now?

She sank down on the mattress. What was going on here? Was he only pretending to be reasonable and cooperative? Was he putting on an act? Her throat tightened. This was all too awful to even consider. There was only one way to solve it. She had to ask him.

Did she dare? What if he exploded? What if he went after her?

No. No. She was being overly dramatic again. She was shaking now, but she stood up, clutching the envelope and the letters in her hand. She couldn't stay in Marksville with him and not know. She couldn't.

Whatever the truth, she had to ask him. She left the dust rag on his bed and went downstairs and outside. She scanned the fields and saw him on the northern edge. Taking a big breath, she plunged into the rows of thigh-high corn, making her way carefully through the rustling green toward her father. He saw her coming halfway there.

His expression tightened. Was he feeling poorly again? Or did he somehow know what she was going to ask?

"*Dat?*"

"Be careful where you're stepping," he said. She bit back a retort. She'd spent every summer of her life in the fields. She knew how to walk through them without harming anything. "What is it?" he continued.

His eyes lowered to the letters she held in her hand. His eyes widened, and then she saw his face go blank.

She thrust the letters out toward him. "What's this?"

"How should I know?" He looked at the letters in her hand curiously now. "Letters?"

"From Hollybrook. Josh and the kids."

He blanched, and then he put on a smile. "*Ach,* there it is. *Jah,* that envelope came for you, and—"

"You never told me. You never gave it to me." There was accusation in her voice even though she tried to keep it at bay.

He flinched only slightly. "Of course, I didn't. I misplaced it. Where did you find it?" His face was open now, innocent.

It threw her off. "I-I found it in your room."

"Goodness, Lucy. Are you snooping through my things now?"

She took a half step back, abashed. "What? *N-Nee.* I was only dusting and I, well, I found it." How was she suddenly on the defensive? She had done nothing wrong.

He took the envelope and the letters from her. She wanted to snatch them back. They weren't meant for his eyes, and she felt possessive of them. She started to reach out to take them back and then realized she would only make things worse. She waited while he looked at the drawings and read Josh's note.

"So, the *kinner* miss you." He held out the letters and she quickly took them. "Don't sound like he's missing you much."

She sucked in a breath.

"I would think if he was your fiancé, he'd be ... well, it don't sound like a fiancé letter to me."

"We are engaged, *Dat.* We were going to be married this week, but I came here instead."

He looked about to retort but hesitated and took in a slow breath. "I'm awful glad you came, Lucy. It's only because of you that I'm able to be out here working today. I thank you." He nodded toward the letters in her hand. "And Josh and all. I'm right glad it was fine with him that you came."

Turmoil churned through her. This new father confused her completely. Was he serious? Was he grateful? She heard his words, but something was off. And had he really misplaced the envelope? It seemed right odd to her.

"I'm glad you found it. The letters, I mean. And I'm sorry for losing it. Careless of me." He wasn't exactly smiling at her, but he wasn't glaring, and he didn't look angry.

"I truly wasn't snooping, *Dat*," she said, hearing the tremor in her voice, which irritated her. She was on the defensive—like she had been for a good portion of the last five years. It didn't feel good; in truth, she hated feeling like this.

"*Nee*," he said with a chuckle. "I don't know why I said that. Just teasing, I s'pose. But no harm done. You found the letter. I reckon you'll be writing back?"

"The ... the *kinner* will be expecting me to," she said.

"Then you should get at it." He turned to survey his fields. "I need to get back to work." He nodded at her and turned and walked away.

Lucy stood for a moment longer, wondering what had just happened. And then she turned and walked slowly back to the house. She couldn't shake the feeling she'd just participated in some grand play, and her father was somehow the villain. But if what he'd said was true, then he wasn't a villain at all. And he had encouraged her to write back, which was jarring.

She took a deep breath. In any case, she would take his suggestion and write back to the children right then. She could draw pictures for them, too.

And Josh?

Her father's words had hurt because he was right. Josh's letter gave no indication they were engaged—indeed, that there was any kind of tender feeling between them.

"This is what you agreed to," she muttered to herself. "This is the way it will be if you marry him. Are you really wanting this?"

She bit her lip and fought the tears that burned in her eyes. She'd never wanted romance, so why did this bother her so much? If this was what it felt like to love someone, then she had been right in the first place. She would be better off if she never married at all.

But the thought that Josh would then marry someone else— for he would, and she knew it—was simply too disturbing to even consider. No. If he was to marry, it would be to her.

Her heart ached as she went into the house and headed for the bureau to get paper and pencil and an envelope. She sat at the dining table and quickly drew some sketches of a farm and animals for David, and a kite flying in the sky for Cornelia. Then she stared at the blank piece of paper for Josh for a very long time. Finally, she began to write.

*Dear Josh,*

*Thank you for your letter. I miss all of you, too.*

. . .

There, at least she was including him.

*Dat is some better. He is out in the fields today for the first time. I have tried to convince him to go to an* Englisch *doctor, but he isn't in favor.*

*Give your mother my regards. I'm not sure when I'm coming back yet.*

*Lucy*

Lucy read over what she'd written. Goodness, but her letter wasn't any better than his. Should she add something to it? At least sign it, *Your fiancée?*

Her hand was poised over the paper, ready to write more, to add those words at least, but she couldn't do it. She felt too embarrassed. How could she be more affectionate in her letter than he was in his? She felt ridiculous. He'd made it clear they were marrying only to save her from going home. She couldn't change the agreement halfway through.

And besides, she was at home, and she was doing all right. It hadn't been perfect, but it had been miles better than before. It truly did seem that her father had changed. He was clearly making an effort to be more pleasant. She wasn't as on edge as before—or at least it was much less than before.

She believed he had been ill, too, not pretending or tricking her. He wasn't as laid up as she had assumed, but it had been clear from the state of things around the house and barn he hadn't been keeping up.

It wouldn't be so bad to stay on, she realized.

But she had given Josh her promise. And she missed him and the *kinner*. Would she get over it if she didn't return? Surely, it would be acceptable to break her promise if she had to take care of her family. That was probably the only acceptable reason.

She quickly folded her letter and the drawings and put them in the envelope. She addressed it to Cornelia, knowing Cornelia would get a big kick out of that. She got up and found a stamp in the drawer and stuck it in the corner. She walked outside, the hot afternoon sun blaring down on her *kapp*. She glanced behind her toward the fields and saw her father busy at work. He looked fine, and she was glad. He didn't seem to be lagging at all. She had worried that his first day outside would drain him.

She walked to the end of the drive and stuck the letter inside the metal mailbox, raising its red flag. The postman hadn't come that day yet, so this letter could get to Josh as soon as tomorrow.

She turned back toward the house, pondering what to fix for supper that evening. She could serve left-overs, but she decided it would be nice to serve her father something new. He did love stuffed potatoes, and there were plenty of potatoes in the cellar from last year. There also were onions and cheese. Stuffed potatoes along with some slices of roast beef would make a fine meal.

That settled, she walked a bit more quickly to the house. She'd need to get started right away to have it ready in an hour and a half's time.

# Chapter Twenty-Four

When Bartholomew came in for supper, he stomped loudly in the washroom and then entered the kitchen slowly, his shoulders slumped.

"Something smells right *gut*," he said without much energy.

Lucy stared at him. What had happened between when she'd observed him in the fields all perky and active and now? He seemed like a different man altogether.

"You feeling poorly again?" she asked.

He nodded. "Worked too long, I reckon." He sloughed his way to the kitchen table and sat down.

"Do you need to lie down?" she asked, concerned at the look of utter fatigue on his face.

"*Nee,* daughter. I'm fine."

She turned away to serve the meal, deciding that eating there in the kitchen would be easier since her dad was already seated. She carried the food from the counter to the table, studying her father's face each time she drew near. He looked up at her with the most pathetic expression, and it tore at her heart strings.

They ate mostly in silence. She hesitated to chat much as she wanted her father to conserve his energy. When the meal was over, he pushed back his chair and stood.

"Thank you for the meal," he said and patted his belly.

"You're welcome," she responded in wonder. He never used to thank her for preparing his meals.

And then something happened. For the barest flicker, for the merest fraction of a second, something in his expression changed. There was a look, a hint of satisfaction—almost a gloating. Something in Lucy recoiled—a quick, disturbing thought filling her mind. A wave of unease and distrust swept through her. She stared at him, but the look was gone, and he was now moving away from the table and leaving the room.

She sat very still, hardly able to breathe. Surely, she was mistaken. Surely, she had seen nothing on his face.

But she *had.*

Feeling as if she were about to pass out, she managed to breathe in shallow, quick gasps. Her chest felt as if it would burst. A cold knot formed in her stomach.

Her father was deceiving her. He wasn't ill. Or he wasn't as ill as he claimed.

She was going to be sick. She staggered up from the table and then looked around as if lost. How could he? How could he have stooped so low?

Tears flooded her eyes. She thought of Josh. Of the suspicion in his eyes when she'd told him her father was ill. Of how annoyed she'd gotten with him.

*Ach,* dearest Lord. He'd been right.

She needed to get out of here. She grasped the back of her chair. No. No. Maybe she was being overly dramatic. Maybe she was wrong. Had she manufactured that look because what she really wanted was to go back to Hollybrook and to Josh and the *kinner*?

She needed to be wise about this. She needed to be watchful. If she was careful, she would see more evidence that her father was tricking her.

*Dear* Gott, *help me,* she cried inwardly. *Guide me in what to do.*

The next day, Josh held Lucy's letter in his hand and read it for the fourth time—which certainly didn't take long. Goodness, but it was one of the shortest letters he'd ever received. She hadn't said much at all. Except that she didn't know when she was returning. He read that sentence again, and again felt a punch to his stomach. She was changing her mind. He could hear it just as clearly as if she'd stated it straight out. He had lost her. Just like that. Just so quickly.

He'd had a bad feeling when she told him she was returning home. He'd wanted to argue with her then, but she seemed quite irritable about it. And defensive, so he hadn't said anything really. And now his fears had come true.

She wasn't going to come back. How in the world was he going to break the news to Cornelia and David? They were going to be heartbroken all over again. And his mother... *Ach*, but she was going to be full of, "I told you so's." He wasn't in the mood to hear it.

He wasn't in the mood for much of anything at that moment. He jumped from his chair and stomped up the stairs toward his room.

"That you?" came his mother's voice.

He stopped, annoyed. He hadn't known she'd be up here. Goodness, it wasn't evening yet, and she didn't make the trip up the stairs any more than she absolutely had to. He went to her bedroom door and poked his head inside.

"It's me."

She was sitting on the edge of her bed, and she patted the spot beside her. "Your face looks like an angry rooster who's lost his hens."

He cringed and debated whether he should enter the room or not.

"Son?" she said sharply. "Get in here."

He quickly stuffed the letter into the back waistband of his trousers, not wanting her to see it. He stepped into the room.

"I know Lucy wrote," Tamar announced. "The *kinner* already were up here showing me the drawings." She chuckled. "And that Cornelia. Gracious, but she was pleased the envelope was addressed to her."

"Why are you upstairs before supper?"

"Don't you try to change the subject, son. And besides, this is my home. I can come up here if I want to." Her eyes were piercing. "So. What did she say?"

"They were just drawings, *Mamm*."

"Don't be impertinent. I know you got a letter." She scrutinized him. "That bad, huh?"

He sighed but didn't respond.

"I told you to go get her. You never listen to me, do you." She held out her hand. "Let me read it."

"It weren't to you."

She clucked her tongue. "I know that. Hand it over."

He knew she'd give him no peace until he did, so he pulled the letter from his waistband and handed it to her. She took her time unfolding it and pressing it flat on her lap.

"Well, it certainly ain't very long. Didn't have much to say to you, did she?"

He scowled.

"She ain't coming back," his mother announced.

"She didn't say so."

"And I can tell from your tone you agree with me." Tamar sighed heavily. "The *kinner* are counting the days. And son, I hate to admit it, but I'm no fool. You were right. I do need help."

"I know you do—"

"And I'm not about to adjust to someone else at this point. You need to get that girl back."

"I won't force her."

Tamar threw up her hands. "*Ach,* but you're a stubborn one. As it is, you aren't forcing her. You aren't doing a thing. You aren't even asking her. That snake of a father has done some kind of spell on her."

Josh's eyes widened. His mother didn't usually talk like that. Why, it was bordering on talking about the devil himself.

"Wipe that look off your face," Tamar snapped. "You can go tomorrow and fetch her back."

Josh jumped off the bed. "I ain't going to do that." She pushed too hard, his mother. He was a grown man. He'd lived away from home for years without her telling him what to do. No need to start that again. He wasn't a child.

"You'll lose her for *gut*."

"If it's *Gott's* will, it will work out." He took a deep breath. "This is her choice, *Mamm*. I ain't going to force her."

Tamar shook her head. "But she don't know how you feel."

He chest tightened. *He* didn't even know how he felt half the time. All he knew was that he wasn't going to force Lucy to do anything. She'd had enough of that in her life, and he wasn't about to do it to her, too. No. This was her choice.

"You going to write her back?"

He shrugged. He'd planned to, but he didn't have to tell his mother. She was getting on his nerves, yapping at him.

"You'd better," she said.

"Do you need anything?" he said, changing the subject. "I can fix us some sandwiches for supper."

She sighed heavily. "*Nee.* I'll come back down. Nellie will help me make sandwiches."

*Nellie?* His mother had called Cornelia, *Nellie.* She hadn't done that before. *Ach,* it wasn't Lucy's father who was casting spells. It was Lucy herself.

The very idea made him chuckle. Lucy would be aggravated to hear his thoughts right then, which only made him chuckle all the harder.

"What are you laughin' about, *Dat?*" Cornelia asked when he got downstairs.

"Nothing really."

"When's Lucy coming back?"

"*Ach*, Cornelia. You ask me that every five minutes. I don't know anything more about it. She'll come when she comes." *If she comes,* he thought ruefully.

"You got a letter. What'd she say?"

"She said she misses you."

Cornelia made a face. "We miss her, too. I bet her *dat* is all well now."

David had wandered to join them. "He could come."

Cornelia looked at him. "You're right." She turned to Josh. "He could come here. Then she wouldn't have to be gone."

"*Ach*, both of you, enough talk about it. Cornelia, your *mammi* wants help making sandwiches."

Cornelia perked up. "She does? I can make sandwiches."

"I wanna help," David said.

Cornelia shook her head. "*Nee. Mammi* wanted me, not you. You can help *Dat*."

David looked expectantly at Josh. "Fine," Josh said. "Let's head outside."

In truth, he wanted to sit right down and write Lucy a letter, but that would have to wait. Besides, what was he planning on telling her, anyway?

As he and David walked out to the barn, he toyed with the idea of visiting Lucy. He could say he was there to purchase something from the farm. Or he could say someone had a horse for sale in the area or something. He scoffed. Lucy would see right through both those excuses. They were ridiculous, and she would know it.

He could just tell her he missed her.

He rejected the idea at once. She didn't need that kind of pressure.

But was it really pressure? And did he miss her? He gave a huge sigh. Of course, he missed her. He thought about her entirely too much. She was his first thought in the morning and his last thought at night.

He missed her laughter, and the way his children laughed so much more when she was around. Lucy was good for them. Good for all of them.

But were they good for her? He hoped so. *Ach,* but how he hoped so.

Maybe, he needed to rethink everything and go fetch her back just like his mother had told him to.

## Chapter Twenty-Five

Lucy felt horrible: underhanded and sneaky. But she couldn't help herself. She had to know the truth. She watched every move her father made. Two days had passed since that telling expression on his face, and so far, she had seen nothing more to give her pause.

That morning, he'd come down to breakfast, moving slowly, as if in pain. When she'd questioned him, he'd only said, "Some better this morning."

Which didn't mean anything to her, since she didn't know how ill he was at all. She decided that at the noon meal that day, she would broach the possibility of going back to Hollybrook to see how he responded. She could even revisit getting someone in to help.

She didn't mention Greta or her aunt and uncle, for she knew her father had gone sour on the lot of them. He knew Greta had told her about the job, and he wasn't one to forgive and forget. Lucy missed Greta, but she decided not to spend time with her so as not to risk her father's ire.

And then it dawned on her. Once again, her father's moods were dictating her life. She yearned to go back to Hollybrook, to the new life she was building. She yearned to go back to Josh. If only he wanted her—for more than her service to his family.

She sighed. Wasted emotion, she told herself. Things were as they were. Her moaning about it wasn't going to change anything. But even so, she could go back to Hollybrook. She liked the community. Even if things didn't work out with Josh, she could stay on and find other employment.

By noon, she had a steaming meal of fried chicken, mashed potatoes, green beans, and biscuits on the table. Her father came in right on time, took off his heavy shoes, washed his hands and padded to the table.

"How's it going out there, *Dat?*"

He shrugged. "All right."

"Well, sit on down. The meal will get cold."

She saw the look of satisfaction on his face as he surveyed the table. Lucy joined him in silent prayer and then waited until he helped himself to the food. She then filled her plate too, although her nerves were jangling, and she didn't know how much she could actually eat.

"I, uh, wanted to talk to you about something," she ventured.

He looked up from his plate. His hand paused over the mashed potatoes. "*Jah?*"

"You seem to be doing much better these days. I'm glad for it, *Dat*," she added, putting on a smile. "And I'm glad that I came back to help you." She swallowed. "But I think it's time for me to return."

She dared look at him. His expression had frozen.

She hurried on. "You know I was about to get married, and I've put off Josh long enough." Did Josh even care about that? She had no real idea, but it was her excuse to leave, and she was going to use it. Wasn't that why Josh had proposed to her in the first place?

"You're going to leave me?" His voice was even, but she could tell he was putting in effort to keep it that way.

"Um. *Jah, Dat*. I … I made a promise."

"A promise?" He was slipping—his voice went up a notch.

"*Jah*. To Josh." She pressed her back against the wooden chair. She only barely kept herself from flinching in dread.

269

"And what about me?" he asked. He was blinking rapidly, and Lucy could see what it was costing him to try to keep his voice level.

"You're doing so much better." She attempted a smile, but it fell flat. "And... And, we can get some help to cook and clean."

He laid down his fork with pointed care. He looked up at her, his face set. "You are my daughter. You've come home to help me. I still need help."

"But you're feeling so much better!"

"Don't you tell me how I feel."

"But you even said—"

"And don't put words in my mouth," he said, his voice now harsh. "I'll tell you when I don't need you anymore. I'll decide when and if you go back."

She gaped at him and even he looked flustered. He'd said too much, and he clearly knew it.

"I mean..." he tried to backtrack. "When I feel better. I mean, maybe you could stay until I'm fully well."

"*Dat*." She was trembling inside but was determined that he wouldn't see it. "You're better. But you do need someone to cook and clean. I'll start asking around. I have some names in mind, like I told you before."

His hands were clenched on the table. She didn't move, refusing to be cowed. She could hardly believe she was in the same situation as before. Was she really so foolish as to keep repeating what she disliked so fervently?

"I don't want anyone else," he said, his voice tight. "I have a daughter. Even the deacon agreed with me on this. *You* should be here, helping me."

"That was before the deacon knew I was engaged," she said.

Her father was staring at her now in a way that unnerved her. She had a sick feeling in her stomach for she knew exactly what he was going to say next.

"You weren't engaged before my visit, *were you?* That was all put on for the deacon's benefit."

She didn't flinch. Indeed, she didn't even blink. Was she to lie now? There was no other way out…

She drew in a long, deep breath and stood up. "I can't believe you would even ask me such a thing." Not a lie, exactly. She prayed her voice didn't quiver, didn't reveal just how shaken she was.

His eyes narrowed further, but before he could say more, she left the room, her shoulders erect and her chin up. Once she cleared the door, she nearly collapsed, but she kept walking, straight up the stairs to her room.

She went to her bed and sat down, thoroughly disgusted now. She was a grown woman. She had gained her freedom once, and yet here she was. Had she learned nothing?

She pressed her hand to her mouth and shook her head. She shouldn't have come. But that would have meant ignoring everything she'd been taught growing up. Bartholomew Oyer was her father, and she had been raised to obey him. But she wasn't so sure of her upbringing anymore. Hadn't the spirit of the teaching been violated by her father?

Didn't that free her? Didn't that release her? Had she truly been taught to put herself under her father's authority no matter what?

And to remain there as a grown adult?

She stood up and walked to her window, looking out over the yard, now tidy since she'd weeded the flower beds. Her thoughts were jumbled, but for the first time in her life, she considered carefully her childhood teaching. She thought beyond the apparent meaning to the real spirit of the teaching. And when she did that, she could see no way she was obligated to continue under her father's authority.

She gazed to the heavens. It would be so much easier if God would suddenly come down and visit with her in the flesh. But hadn't Jesus sent his Holy Spirit? Wasn't that sufficient?

"*Gott?* I don't want to displease You," she whispered. "But I want to leave my father, leave my home. I want to go back and stay in Hollybrook."

She leaned her head against the glass pane of her window. She stood very still, listening, hoping to hear something. But she heard nothing. She didn't even hear anything from her father downstairs. She wondered what he was doing, whether he was still sitting at the table.

She stood there until her heart slowed and her breathing became more or less normal. As she waited, listening, she began to feel better. Her tension eased, and she felt a glimmer of hope. She was going to leave. She was going to return to Hollybrook. Maybe not tomorrow, but the next day. She'd work tomorrow, cook all day, and freeze up some meals for her father. She didn't mind doing that; indeed, she was glad for it. Making those meals could be her last parting gift to him.

She wouldn't find help for him, though. If he wasn't in favor, she could only guess at the kind of treatment he would give the poor woman. Better for him to hire someone later if he changed his mind.

Her heart fluttered with some excitement now. She would see Josh and the children and Tamar soon.

*Josh.*

She had tried to lessen her affection for him, but it hadn't worked. If anything, she yearned for him even more. Would she still marry him? By this time next week, would she be a married woman?

At the thought, something intense flared through her.

*Ach, Josh, can't you want me for yourself, too?* her heart cried. *Isn't there some part of you who wants me?*

∽

It was much later when Lucy dared go back downstairs. Her father was nowhere to be found. She peered through the kitchen window and thought she saw movement in the barn. So much for him needing to lie down and rest. She was certain now he had been exaggerating everything to get her to come home. She didn't need more evidence; she simply *knew*.

She made quick work of cleaning up the kitchen, putting the leftovers into plastic containers and into the fridge. Then she took stock of what supplies there were. She should make a fast run to the mercantile in the morning and pick up some more supplies, so she'd have something to work with in making so many meals. She opened the freezer and saw that it wasn't full. Good. There was room for her to put the pre-cooked meals when they were ready.

Feeling better with each moment that passed, she decided to spend the rest of the evening upstairs. She didn't want to risk another confrontation with her father. She pulled her suitcase out from under her bed. She could pack everything but the dress and undergarments she'd need for the next day and a half. With every item she packed, she felt more and more peace and contentment. As she closed her suitcase and slid it back under the bed, she thought again of God and the Holy Spirit.

"Is this how You're telling me?" she asked in a soft voice. "With this peace I feel?"

She smiled. She may not have heard God's audible voice, but there was no mistaking the feeling in her heart. She prayed for her father then, that he could experience this same peace. And then she got out her Bible and began to read.

~

Josh was going. He'd bid the children farewell and his mother, too. He'd told them he would be back before nightfall. His mother had given him a smug knowing look which had nearly made him change his mind. But then, he scolded himself for being so immature. Besides, he was set on his mission now. He was going to convince Lucy to come back, even if it meant bringing her cranky father with her.

During the night, he'd done some major soul-searching. He still grieved his Sara, and he always likely would. But Sara was gone, and he wasn't. Neither were his two beautiful children. And they were crazy about Lucy.

As was he.

He sat on the bus and couldn't help smiling. It was good to see his way clear. It felt clean and fresh and new. And happy. He hadn't felt like this for ages it seemed.

*Please, Lucy, want to come back. Please.*

"You going on vacation?" asked the elderly woman sitting beside him.

Josh gave a start, surprised she was talking to him. She hadn't said a word when she first sat down beside him at the bus stop.

"Me? *Ach, nee.*"

She nodded. "Just tending to some business, then?"

"I s'pose you could put it like that."

Her sharp grey eyes traveled down his clothes. "You're Amish," she said, stating the obvious.

"That I am."

"I've always had an infinity toward the Amish," she said. She folded her hands in her lap. "I had a great-great-grandmother who was Amish." She looked at him and laughed. "At least, that's what they tell me."

She looked at him expectantly, and he had no idea what she was wanting him to say, so he only smiled.

"Yes, that's what they tell me. I'm old as dirt, of course. Well, you can see that since you have eyes in your head. I've often wondered what life would be like if I was Amish." She tilted her head. "You think I could have made it, being Amish?"

*Ach*, what a question.

"If you decided to."

She laughed again. "Good answer. But I do love my television. They have game shows on every evening at seven o'clock. I don't think I could go to sleep without watching my game shows first. I'm quite good, you know. I do believe I could win them if I ever went on television."

"I ... I see."

She giggled. "Me on television. At my age. I think I'd be quite the person to watch."

"I'm sure you would." His mind was still stuck on game shows. What kind of game shows? He had no idea what she was talking about.

She reached over and patted his arm. "You seem like a real nice man. I hope your business goes well."

His mind flipped back to Lucy. "Me, too."

"I'll leave you alone. I know I can get to talking too much. I don't figure you need to hear everything I have to say." She smiled, and he noted she had one front tooth nearly broken clean off. He wondered if it had hurt when it happened. "Anyway, the best of luck to you."

"Thank you." He returned her smile, glad for some silence again, as he was wanting to think about what he'd say when he saw Lucy. He hoped she'd answer the door and not her father. He wanted to speak with her first. He'd practiced what he would say in the night, but in the bright light of morning, it didn't sound nearly as good as it had in the night.

He needed to rethink it, and they were over halfway there. He closed his eyes and tried to envision seeing Lucy again. He tried to figure out what to say, but nothing came.

*All right, dear* Gott. *Please give me the words I'll need*, he finally prayed, giving up.

## Chapter Twenty-Six

Lucy had gone to the mercantile and bought quite a few groceries. She put them on her father's tab, as she didn't have that much money with her. She'd made breakfast that morning and set it out for her father. He'd come in, said nothing, and wolfed it down. Then he stood abruptly and headed outside through the washroom.

Once she heard the screen door bang, she'd gone to the window and watched him. He was moving in his normal fashion and looked to be feeling fine. So, he wasn't even making a pretense now.

She swallowed the bitterness that rose up, knowing it wouldn't do her a lick of good. She was determined to leave her childhood home the next day without rancor. She wasn't going to allow her father to color her mood or her new life. She would do her best to only think of him with compassion, if not sympathy.

Hurting people hurt others. She remembered her mother saying this once after being belittled by another woman at a quilting bee. Lucy had never forgotten it, nor had she forgotten how her mother seemed to be able to let it go. That was what Lucy wanted. To let all this awfulness go. To be free of it.

She spread all her groceries over the counter to decide what to do first. She planned to make at least three casseroles and to divide them into servings and freeze them. She would also make a fresh salad and bread. If she made four loaves, she could freeze three of them.

Lucy also planned to thoroughly clean the house; but in truth, it didn't need much. She'd been keeping up with the cleaning since she'd arrived.

She was well into making the second casserole when she heard someone knock on the front screen. How odd. She hadn't heard any buggy approaching, and she usually did since the drive was gravel. She wiped her hands quickly on a dish towel and went to the open door.

As she neared it, she jerked to a stop, her eyes wide as she gaped through the door and the screen. *Josh?* Josh Lambright was *here?*

And then she flew to the screen door, throwing it open.

"*Ach*, Josh! What is it? Has something happened to one of the *kinner*? Is it your mother?" The words tumbled from her mouth as fear gripped her heart.

"*Nee, nee*," he said quickly, taking a step closer to her. "The *kinner* are fine. *Mamm* is fine."

She let out her breath in a rush. "*Ach*, you frightened me."

So ... the family was fine? Then, why was he there? Her mind whirled, trying to make sense of it.

"You're ... likely wondering why I'm here," he said, taking off his straw hat and fingering its brim nervously. "I, well, I..."

She waited. Why was he so nervous? Something had to be wrong.

"Is your father in the fields?" he asked, peering around her to glance into the house.

"*Jah*."

"So he's better?"

She slumped, feeling foolish. Dare she tell him the truth? That he had been right all along? That she'd been misled about the whole situation?

When she didn't answer, he went on. "I'm right glad he's better. It makes this easier..."

281

"Makes what easier?"

Her heart was racing now. He was standing close to her, so close she could easily reach out and touch his dear face. And she wanted to. She wanted to touch him, to feel him, to breathe him in. The intensity of her feelings shocked and unnerved her. She could feel tears burning the backs of her eyes, but she didn't dare allow them to fall. She felt vulnerable and frightened. If she felt this strongly for him—if she loved him—then she was opening herself to the possibility of pain, and she didn't want that. She'd worked to avoid that.

Yet, here she was—standing before him, completely in love with him.

He was watching her and seemed to be weighing the expressions on her face. He took another step closer and then hesitated. "Lucy...?"

She blinked. "*Jah?*"

"I came because I had to." Again, he hesitated, searching her face. "I want you to come home." He raised his hand. "I'm not telling you. I'm not demanding that you come. I'm not your father. I just ... I just want you to come."

She swallowed past the lump in her tight throat. She finally managed to eke out, "Why?"

He licked his lips and his eyes bore into hers with a power that took her breath. "Because I love you."

## THE RECENT WIDOWER

She sucked in her breath. "*What?* What did you say?"

He reached out and grasped her shaking hand in his. "I said, I love you."

"B-but ... you love Sara."

He gave her a tender smile. "*Jah,* I do. And I will always love Sara. I will. But she's gone, Lucy. And I-I love you. And Lucy..." He tossed his hat onto a porch rocking chair and took her second hand in his. "My love for you stands, having nothing to do with Sara."

She frowned only slightly as she pondered his words. Could it be true? That he loved her? That he wanted her for her? Not just for the children and the household and his mother? She looked into his eyes. Was there an ulterior motive there? Was she only hearing what she wanted to hear?

"You're doubting me, *ain't so?*" he asked gently. "It's all right. But you'll see, if you give me a chance. Is there... is there any chance at all you have feelings for me? Do you think you could grow to love me? Are you willing to give us a chance?"

His words sank into her heart, filling an emptiness that had grown deeper with every year that passed. She gazed into his eyes and saw his tears, and then she began to cry. He sucked in his breath and pulled her to him, running his hand down her head and over her back, comforting her.

"*Ach,* Lucy," he muttered into her *kapp.* "What is it? Are you all right? What is it?"

She pulled away and looked into his eyes. "I just... I just can't believe..." She sniffed. "I ... I love you, too. I never wanted to, but I do." And she started crying again.

He chuckled warmly now and pulled her close again. "Dearest Lucy. I guess we're stuck with each other."

She put her arms around him and held him close. "I... I guess we are."

They held each other for a long while. Lucy's breathing slowed as she felt the beating of his heart against her cheek, steady and strong. He was really there, and he loved her. Everything was all right. She could trust him. She knew it to be true, deep in her soul, and it was such a good, warm knowing that she basked in it, feeling its warmth, its love.

"Josh?"

"*Jah?*"

"I was going to return to Hollybrook tomorrow."

He pulled away and smiled down at her. "Were you? Truly?"

"I was. I, well, I didn't know about us getting married. I didn't want you to marry me only to help me escape my father. I wanted you to want me."

"I do want you," he interrupted her. He leaned down and kissed her cheek, and then his lips moved slowly to her mouth, and he touched her lips gently, sweetly. A thrill raced through her.

"I do want you," he repeated.

"And I want you," she whispered. She still could hardly believe he was there. That he loved her. That he wanted her. That they would be married after all.

"Can you come back with me today?" he asked.

She pulled away. "I'm cooking food to put in the freezer for *Dat*. I planned to clean the house, too, from top to bottom."

"Does he know you're leaving?"

She nodded. "I told him." She drew in a long breath. "You were right."

He gave her a quizzical look. "About what?"

"He wasn't as sick as he let on. He... He has been making it seem worse. Deceiving me."

Josh shook his head. "*Ach,* I'm sorry. I'm so sorry. I didn't want to be right."

"I should have known," she said. "But he's my *dat*."

Josh took her hand. "It's all right. He's your *dat,* and you love him. You want to believe the best of him."

"But I was wrong."

He nodded. "I'm so sorry."

She straightened her spine. "Well, now I know. And I want to do this. The meals, I mean. I want to leave the freezer fully stocked, and I want to leave the house completely clean."

"Tell me what to do."

She gaped at him. "What?"

"I'll help you. I'm here, aren't I? I want to help."

"But ... but this is woman's work."

He laughed. "I don't care. Put me to work. I know how to use a broom. And I'm not awful in the kitchen. When Sara died, I had to do it all."

She gazed at this amazing man, and her heart swelled with love for him. "*Jah*, you did have to do it all," she said softly.

"So, why don't I start sweeping and dusting and you can keep cooking."

She smiled. "All right. If you insist."

He pulled her close and kissed her again. "I insist. I can't wait to take you home."

"What will your mother think?"

He laughed. "She's all for it, let me tell you. She wanted me to come fetch you."

"Did she truly?"

He laughed again. "She truly did."

"Then I guess we better get busy. The broom is in the washroom."

Together, they got down to business. Lucy's heart soared when she finished fixing all the meals. Her father didn't come in for the noon meal, which was highly unusual. She nearly went out to call him in but decided against it. She wondered if he knew Josh was there. She doubted it as Josh had walked to the farm from the bus stop. So unless he'd been watching, there was no way for him to know.

Just as well, for Lucy had no idea how he would react.

"Sweeping and dusting are done," Josh announced, coming into the kitchen. "*Ach*, it smells heavenly in here."

Lucy handed him a full plate. "I saved a piece for you. Consider it payment for all the work you're doing."

He chuckled and took the plate. "This isn't necessary but is much appreciated. You coming home with me is all the payment I need." His eyes were tender on hers. She shook her head slightly, not accustomed to hearing such kind and loving words. Inwardly, she smiled. She'd better get used to it, though, for she was marrying this wonderful man.

"I'm so eager to see the *kinner*."

"They're just as eager to see you. I didn't tell them where I was going today. I was afraid if you wouldn't come back with me, they would be too disappointed."

"You feared I wouldn't come back?"

He nodded solemnly. "I feared it. I didn't know if you cared for me—I, well, I prayed you did."

"I didn't know you cared for me."

"At first, I didn't. I wasn't open to caring for anyone besides Sara." He shrugged. "But I was wrong. Sara would never expect me to put myself on a shelf for her benefit. Sara was a wonderful woman—you would have liked her—and she would want me to marry you. I'm quite certain of it."

"I wish I could have known her."

"I do, too." He smiled at her. "Things are different now."

"I don't expect you to stop loving her. I know you always will."

He exhaled. "Thank you. *Jah,* I always will, but a person can love more than one person. That's what I've been learning. What *Gott* is showing me."

"And what *Gott* is showing me..." she hesitated for only a second, "is that there are men who are trustworthy." She looked at him with tears glistening in her eyes. "Like you. I can trust you."

He pulled her into his arms. "I will do everything I can to be trustworthy."

She sniffed. "You already have."

~

It was three o'clock when Bartholomew came into the house. He stopped short when he saw Josh sitting at the kitchen table.

"When did you get here?" he asked loudly. His eyes shifted to Lucy. "Did you ask him to come?"

"*Nee, Dat*," Lucy said, forcing herself to remain calm. "He came to fetch me, as our wedding date is around the corner."

"Your *wedding date*," he said sarcastically.

Josh stood. "I love your daughter dearly," he said, his voice surprisingly amiable. "I simply couldn't wait any longer to see her and take her home to marry her."

Bartholomew blinked. His eyes went back and forth between them. "You don't need to pretend anymore. I know it was all fake."

"Pretend?" Lucy questioned, her ire rising. "You mean like pretending to be sick."

As soon as the words were out of her mouth, she wanted to snatch them back. She sounded peevish and spiteful, and that wasn't who she wanted to be. She felt her cheeks flame with color.

"*Ach*, I-I'm sorry. Please forget I said that." Ashamed, she looked at Josh, fearing to see censure in his eyes, but all she saw was compassion.

"We'd be happy to have you attend the wedding," Josh said, as if they were all having a friendly chat on a sunny afternoon. "I'm sure Lucy would like her father to be there. Then you can spend some time with my *kinner* and my *mamm*."

Josh walked to Lucy and took her hand in his. "It will be a small wedding as we're planning it so quickly. Still, we'd be pleased if you would come."

He faced Bartholomew directly as if challenging him to disagree or find fault. Bartholomew's mouth tightened into a straight line. Josh said nothing more, just continued to look at his future father-in-law with a pleasant smile. Lucy was clenching his hand, as if hanging on for dear life.

A look of confusion flashed across Bartholomew's face. He cleared his throat and stared at Lucy. "When are you leaving?"

"We're taking the last bus today."

He winced only slightly. "You better get going, then."

"I've made you a lot of meals," she said quickly, fearing he would cut her off. "They're all packaged in the freezer for you. And I'll call and leave a message on the shanty phone with the exact date of the wedding." She swallowed hard. "Like Josh says ... we'd be right glad to have you."

She wasn't sure if it was true or not. At that moment, she didn't know how she felt about it. She was eager to leave, to not see her father every day, but she did appreciate Josh's generous gesture in inviting him. Then there would be nothing to regret. What her father did with the invitation was up to him.

She wasn't responsible, and the knowledge of that made her feel suddenly lighter. She smiled at her father now, a genuine smile, a sad smile. She took off her dirty apron and folded it over her arm.

"You're right, *Dat*. We need to get going."

"I don't see no buggy."

"We're walking," Josh said. "It won't take long."

For a quick second, Lucy hoped her father would offer to hitch up the buggy and take them, but of course, he didn't. He only gave a grudging grunt and left the room, heading back outside.

Lucy turned to Josh and took a deep breath. She was fighting tears but not sure why. Tears of happiness? Of relief? Of frustration?

She had no idea. Josh put his arm around her. "Are you packed?"

"I am. I, well, I packed earlier for tomorrow. It won't take me but a minute to throw in some last things."

"*Gut.* I'll wait for you down here."

She turned and fled up the stairs, her step now light and eager and only a little nervous.

## Chapter Twenty-Seven

"Lucy!" Cornelia cried, running out of the house. "You're back!"

David was on her heels, also hollering Lucy's name. Lucy raced across the yard to catch them in an embrace.

"*Ach, kinner.* I've missed you so."

"*Mammi* let me do lots of cooking," Cornelia said, grinning. "And me and David did lots of other chores, too, but we liked it. *Dat* did some cooking, but it weren't so *gut*. *Mammi* will be glad to see you."

"Goodness, daughter," Josh said. "Take a breath. Give Lucy a chance to breathe, too."

But Cornelia wasn't having it. She wouldn't let go of Lucy, nor would David. Lucy finally plunked herself right down on the soft grass, and they nearly fell on top of her. They began giggling and tickling each other. Lucy's heart was nearly bursting with joy.

Finally, Josh peeled his children off her, and they all started toward the front door, their arms around one another. The screen door was pushed open and there stood Tamar.

"Tamar," Lucy cried. "It's so *gut* to see you up and about."

Tamar gave a stern nod. "I didn't break my hip. How many times do I have to tell all of you?"

Her voice was severe, but her expression had softened into what looked to be affection. Lucy gave her a wide smile and went to her, giving her a hug.

"It's *gut* to be back."

Tamar made as if to reject Lucy's hug, but she ended up patting her on the back.

"The *kinner* told me you would be glad I'm back," Lucy dared say.

Tamar made a face, but she was clearly holding back a smile. "Don't believe what them *kinner* tell you."

"Never," Lucy said. "I won't believe a word of it."

"*Mammi,* you said so. I heard you," David protested.

"Me, too," Cornelia said. "We all heard you."

Tamar gave a nonchalant shrug, and they all went in the house together.

# Epilogue

*One Year Later*

When I look back on all that happened over the last year, I am left with only gratitude. In truth, I had to work on forgiveness. Mainly for myself. After I left *Dat's*, even though I knew I was doing the right thing, even though I knew *Gott* was blessing me, I sometimes felt guilty. Going against what I'd been taught my whole life was hard.

I had more than one tearful conversation with Josh about it. He was always understanding, never pushy. I know he had to work on forgiving my *dat*, just like I did. It seemed like the first few months of our marriage were all about forgiveness.

*Dat* didn't come to our wedding. I didn't think he would, but it still hurt when he wasn't there. Folks here wondered at that, but Josh said he simply couldn't make it, and though I could see some still had questions, they didn't say anything further. Our wedding was small, but I thought it was beautiful. Tamar helped me make my dress and we also made a new dress for Nellie. *Ach,* but the child was over the moon with excitement. Josh bought a new shirt for David and for himself.

The house wasn't overly full of guests, mostly friends of Tamar. But Greta did come, and I was so happy to see her. We had a tearful reunion, chatting nonstop until almost the time of the service. I didn't really have any attendants, but she stayed close to me as if she were one anyway.

The meal after the wedding was wonderful. The women got together and helped Tamar, and it was delicious—they even managed to produce the traditional creamed celery. I was touched with their generosity and their care, and so was Josh.

We didn't do the usual visiting kin after the wedding, as there was simply too much to do on the farm. Besides, we didn't want to leave Tamar or the *kinner*, so it was just easier to stay home. I know the *Englisch* make quite a fuss over a honeymoon, but I was content to have my "honeymoon" right here at home.

We had a decent crop that summer, which pleased Josh because he felt like he got it in a bit late—what with his move and all. Still, we harvested enough to make a suitable profit for the year to come. And truly, though this sounds right silly, I think we could have lived on nothing. I'd never been so happy in my life.

I told Josh from the beginning that I knew he was still grieving his first wife, and I understood. He didn't have to rush his grief for me. I think he appreciated that, and there were times—there still are times—when I know he is thinking of Sara and missing her. But it hasn't colored our marriage. He is a wonderful husband, kind and loyal and true.

With each month that passes, I trust him more. I truly never realized how living with my father during those years after *Mamm* died had made me so fearful of others, mainly men. Even though I knew with my head that Josh wasn't like my *dat*, it took a while for my heart to know it and to relax and enjoy being in love.

Now, I can't imagine my life without Josh and the *kinner* and Tamar.

Tamar has endured some struggles this year. She recovered from her fall early on, but then she fell again a couple months later. That time, she wasn't so lucky. Her hip did break. *Ach,* but she hated being in the hospital and all the therapy afterward. But her spirit is as feisty as ever and so is her tongue.

Although, when she aims her tongue at me now, I know it's her frustration, not her dislike of me. We get along well, and in truth, I'm the only one who can cajole her into a better mood. She's getting around a bit now, though with a walker, which she hates. But the *kinner* cater to her and despite her grumpiness, I know she likes it.

## THE RECENT WIDOWER

I've made dear friends here in Hollybrook. This district is special somehow; I'm not sure why. The people are loving and patient and laugh a lot. I like that most of all—the laughter. I didn't realize how seldom I used to laugh. Now, I find myself joking all the time, and I especially love it when I get Josh laughing. His laugh is deep and resonant and contagious. And then the *kinner* get to laughing, and if we're lucky, Tamar will join in.

It's so odd when I remember I used to be a spinster and was glad of it. Now, I'm a married woman with two children and ... one on the way. I'm nearly certain it's true, and I find myself smiling all day long. I plan to go to Old Mae, the local herb woman, and see what she says. I think she'll confirm what I pray is true, and then I'll tell Josh.

I can't wait to see his smile when I tell him. *Ach,* but it will be precious. He'll be as thrilled as I am. And the *kinner*. Nellie will likely run me over with excitement. And David will likely stand there and grin at me in that charming way he has.

When Old Mae confirms it, I will write my *dat,* too, and let him know. Perhaps being a *daadi* will soften his heart. But it will be all right if it doesn't. I'm truly fine with it either way now, which is a miracle of *Gott,* for sure and for certain.

*Ach,* when I think of all *Gott* has done for me, all He has given me, I am so grateful. My heart swells until I think it will burst. Life is *gut* and full of hope. Our future is in *Gott's* hands, exactly where it should be. During our meals, when I glance around the table at those dear faces, sometimes my eyes fill with tears. And of course, Nellie notices.

"What are you cryin' for, *Mamm*?" she'll ask. And then she grins, her mouth stretching wide. "It's cuz you love us, *ain't so*? Them are happy tears, *ain't so*? Like you tell me sometimes."

And I'll nod and grin right back. "*Jah,* Nellie. They're happy tears. And *jah,* I love every one of you."

Then Josh will invariably grab my hand, bring it to his lips, and kiss it.

The End

## Continue Reading...

❦

Thank you for reading **The Recent Widower. Are you wondering what to read next?** Why not read **Searching for Her Baby? Here's a peek for you:**

*Eight Years Before*

Hagar King sat on the hard narrow bed and clutched Enoch's letter to her chest. The edges of the thin piece of paper curled around her fingers, crinkling in her grip. He loved her—he *still loved her*. Not that anyone would believe it. Those in her family said Enoch Yoder was a good-for-nothing. He was only out for mischief. After all, look at the fix he got her in.

Hagar took a slow, deep breath and set Enoch's letter on the quilt beside her. But Enoch Yoder was *not* a good-for-nothing. He was the boy she loved with all her heart. And she missed him more than she ever dreamed possible. She ran her hand over her swollen belly, feeling the child within her kick mightily.

"*Ach*," she whispered, "you're a strong one, that you are."

A footstep sounded on the stairway, and Hagar went stiff. Then she flew into motion quick as a skittering bug—snatching the letter and envelope off her bed and cramming them inside the bedside stand. They were barely out of sight before her aunt, Bernice King, poked her head through the open door.

"What are you doing up here?" Bernice asked, her voice strident as usual. "I'm needing help in the kitchen with the noon meal."

Hagar lowered her eyes meekly for she'd learned such a stance often mollified her aunt. She stood. "*Jah, Aenti*. I'm coming."

She walked to the door, her gait only somewhat ungainly with the extra weight she was carrying. She glanced at her aunt from beneath her lashes and saw the sharp assessing look she was giving her.

"What *were* you doing up here?"

Hagar swallowed and put on her innocent face; the one she had perfected over the last seven months. "Just resting, *Aenti*. I get tired right quick these days."

"And whose fault is that?" Bernice shot back.

Hagar bit her lip and headed down the stairs.

"That boy ain't trying to contact you, is he?" Bernice continued, following at Hagar's heels down the steps.

"How could he?" Hagar asked, keeping her face averted. "He has no idea where I am."

"He'd better not. I'm responsible for you, and I won't have it."

Hagar rolled her eyes, glad her aunt couldn't see her face. "I know."

**VISIT HERE To Read More!**
https://ticahousepublishing.com/amish.html

# Thank you for Reading

※

If you **love Amish Romance, Visit Here:**

https://amish.subscribemenow.com/

to find out about all **New Hollybrook Amish Romance Releases! We will let you know as soon as they become available!**

If you enjoyed ***The Recent Widower,*** would you kindly take a couple minutes to leave a positive review on Amazon? It only takes a moment, and positive reviews truly make a difference. I would be so grateful! Thank you!

**Turn the page to discover more Amish Romances just for you!**

## More Amish Romance for You

**We love clean, sweet, rich Amish Romances and have a lovely library of Brenda Maxfield titles just for you!** (Remember that ALL of Brenda's Amish titles can be downloaded FREE with Kindle Unlimited!)

**If you love bargains, you may want to start right here!**

**VISIT HERE to discover our complete list of box sets!**

https://ticahousepublishing.com/bargains-amish-box-sets.html

**VISIT HERE to find Brenda's single titles.**

https://ticahousepublishing.com/amish.html

## About the Author

I was blessed to live part-time in Indiana, a state I shared with many Amish communities. I now live in Costa Rica. One of my favorite activities is exploring other cultures. My husband, Paul, and I have two grown children and six precious grandchildren. I love to hole up in our mountain cabin and write. You'll also often find me walking the shores by the sea. Happy Reading!

https://ticahousepublishing.com/

Made in the USA
Monee, IL
14 May 2022